Rendezvous at the Populaire

A Novel of Sherlock Holmes

Kate Workman

Paperback ISBN 9781908218704
Mobipocket/Kindle ISBN 9781908218711
ePub ISBN 9781908218728

Published in the UK by MX Publishing
335 Princess Park Manor, Royal Drive, London, N11 3GX
www.mxpublishing.com

Cover artwork by www.staunch.com

First and foremost, I dedicate this to Sir Arthur Conan Doyle, Gaston Leroux, and Andrew Lloyd Weber, without whom I could not have created this book. Also, to fellow author Sam Siciliano for writing the first Phantom and Holmes novel.

On a more personal note, this book is dedicated to my fiancé, Andrew Shainberg. I love you. Thank you for believing in me.

I've loved writing about the two arguably greatest literary characters and I hope this book lives up to its readers' expectations.

Sherlock Holmes

Not long ago, I was searching through many of the papers my dear friend, Dr. Watson, left at my residence. To my surprise, I found numerous notes about the Opera Populaire in Paris, the setting for the most heart-wrenching case of my career.

He wrote often of my distaste for his writing style and what I felt were flowery forms of recollection. However, I find myself wishing now that he'd completed this tale and given it to the public. No one knows the true story and in thinking over things later, I found I wanted people to understand the methods behind the outward madness. Alas, initially, I scolded Watson quite severely and told him to keep his meddling nose out of this story. I wanted no part in it and I insisted that not a word, not even a syllable, should reach the public. He listened to me and immediately ceased his narrative.

Luckily, with his unfortunately rather incomplete notes, some statements and letters from different members of the opera house, and my own keen ability for recollection of the most minute details, I can recreate this tale, giving a full account of the events that transpired, and hand it to the public myself. Of course I must give Watson his proper credit and, as much as it pains me to do so, admit I was an overly cautious fool for not letting him fully record these events for the public eye.

Watson, I believe, paints me as having an ever-growing interest in this case, but in strict denial of that fact. I admit my denial, but an ever-growing interest? Not likely. My interest was immediate, but the situation in which I found myself at the time was not very favourable to taking on a case of such magnitude.

I believe Watson details the accident much better than I, but suffice it to say we were on a chase after my ever-notorious nemesis, Professor Moriarty. It was fruitless, for once again, the wretch eluded my grasp. Yet, in the course of the night, something happened that had never happened before. I was so severely injured that after as much of the recuperative process as could be achieved, I decided to retire my skills as a detective.

However, I am eternally grateful I took on this peculiar mystery. It allowed me to meet someone who is a true musical genius, the likes of which I could only ever dream of achieving, as well as he being someone just as clever and cunning as I. He was a formidable foe, but in the end, one I--

Well, I digress. And I can't thoughtlessly reveal the ending before the beginning is told. I feel I must apologize, for as much as Watson's writings were to my distaste, he maintained a certain continuity to his tales. I'm afraid the segments I narrate will not be anywhere near as smooth. Undoubtedly in the writing, I will switch between perfect detail and recollection of dialogue and description to vague impressions of the events. It is the curse of one such as I, an action taker instead of a patient observer, calmly and meticulously recording the details. And yes, I am aware of a certain irony in that. I suppose it can be argued that I *mentally* script every detail, choreographing it in my mind, for nothing that is important in a case ever escapes my keen eye. I find I have no explanation for this contradiction.

I must confess that the entire collection is labelled instead of chaptered. Watson's writings are set apart by his heading of "From the Journal of . . ." at the top. It was his personal stationery and I rather liked the idea, so I have headed the consequent segments in similar ways, relating to who was involved or what was happening.

Before I digress any further, ladies and gentlemen, I give you the strange affair of the Phantom of the Opera; a mystery never fully explained.

Until now.

From the Journal of John H. Watson, M.D.

It was a Tuesday in the autumn of 1883 when I climbed those seventeen familiar steps and stood at the doorway to Sherlock Holmes's residence at 221B Baker Street. Some distant corner of my mind recalled how I'd discovered there were seventeen steps. Holmes, having just explained his deduction regarding my going back to medical practice, had narrowed down the difference between 'seeing' and 'observing' for me. Of course, to me the words were synonyms, nothing more; however, he gave me an acute example. He asked me how often I'd seen the steps outside the apartment. By then, some hundreds of times, I was sure. So how many were there? I found I couldn't answer. I had not observed that detail.

I smiled ruefully as I reached the top. How I wish there were different circumstances than the ones I faced when climbing these stairs day after day. I'd been visiting my dear friend for an hour or two every day for the past several months, ever since our return from Paris. After the events that transpired in that dreadful and beautiful city, he'd gone into a melancholia so deep, I feared for his safety.

However, as I approached his door that day, I distinctly heard the strains of a violin. Smiling widely, I entered the room and saw a pleasant sight: Holmes standing up, eyes closed, with his weight completely on his left leg, violin positioned under his chin as his thin fingers securely held the bow and drew it over the strings. His silver-headed cane, a now permanent fixture on his person, leaned against the wall, a mere three feet from his grasp.

I sat down in a chair near the door and waited patiently for this solo concert to end so he would notice my arrival. As the notes of his haunting melody settled over my ears, I found I recognized the tune. The memory brought back the harsh beginning of what had spurred Holmes to take the case in Paris . . .

It was a brisk November night in 1882 when England almost lost its greatest detective.

In what he later wished to be his last case, my dear friend, Sherlock Holmes, was shot. It was near midnight, at a dock overlooking the Thames . . .

"Watson, when I give the signal, we run. If my calculations are correct, Moriarty will panic and head to his right, leading him directly to a dead end. That is where we will corner and apprehend him, and his growing reign of terror over the criminal minds of this city shall be ended," Holmes whispered to me as we hid out behind several stacked crates. As always, Holmes had picked an ingenious location, one that enabled us to stand upright instead of being crouched down, or worse, positioned on our knees when he gave his signal to give chase. There is nothing more trying than attempting to run after one's lower legs have completely fallen asleep. I, at least, was more likely to land in a heap after the first step, and Holmes could afford no mistakes tonight.

We waited several tense minutes and then I saw, out of the corner of my eye, Holmes's hand flutter at his side. The signal. We stealthily sneaked around to the front of the crates and then broke into a dead run. At the sound of our footsteps, Moriarty was instantly alerted and, just as Holmes predicted, ran to his right. I almost let out a cry of joy and in my jubilation (because I was still utterly amazed by Holmes's ability to discern peoples' behaviour so accurately,) I fell a few steps behind Holmes.

That was when I heard the gunshot. It came from my left and almost before I could turn to see who had fired, I watched Holmes crash down, skidding on his hands and stomach, to stop on the very edge of the dock, a mere five foot drop separating him from the angry black waters of the Thames.

"Holmes!" I shouted, halting my momentum and throwing myself backwards. The old Jezail bullet wound in my leg protested, and I crumpled to the ground, just out of reach of Holmes.

"Ah, th' boss'll be glad I got one o' you!" I heard behind me. I wrenched my head around, giving myself a frightfully painful neck the next day, and there I saw the gunman, holding a revolver that was pointed at my head.

Normally, that would make anyone pause, or at least take stock of the situation they find themselves in. Perhaps they would try to bargain with the gunman, plead for mercy, or just concede to begging. At any other time, I would be one of those normal individuals. However, I had Holmes, shot, next to me and I knew no time could afford to be wasted. Fast enough that I didn't even realize I was doing it, my fist was sailing toward the man's hand, knocking his grip loose from the gun. Once his weapon had bounced out of his hand and I kicked it off the dock and into the churning water, I got to my knees and pulled him down by the collar of his shirt.

Yes, I was a military doctor, but the important word in that title is not 'doctor.' It is 'military.' I had just as much physical training as any of the soldiers and, despite going through a long recovery after taking a bullet myself, my muscles retained the memory of how to fight. This henchman of Moriarty's did not stand a chance.

I was pummelling him with both fists when I heard a low moan. "Watson . . ." I heard Holmes say weakly.

I started. Holmes! He had to be tended to. I gave the man one last solid punch, coming up on his lower jaw, to assure a state of unconsciousness for several hours. Letting him drop, I crawled over to Holmes. "I'm here. Holmes, I'm here. Where were you hit?"

But almost before I'd asked, I saw it. Holmes had rolled onto his back, revealing his right leg, which was a bloody mess. And I don't mean that as the normal English colloquialism. For several seconds I froze, attempting to make sense of the scene in front of me, but it was hard to get past all that blood gushing from the man I considered to be my closest friend.

"Watson." Holmes forced my name through clenched teeth. "What is . . . the extent . . . of the damage?"

Gulping and releasing a shuddery breath, I forced myself to examine Holmes's leg. With butterfly-soft motions, I moved aside what was left of the material of his pants and inspected his thigh. Torn muscle, bone fragments, and bullet remains were present amidst the decimated skin. His femur was not only broken, but shards of bone were lodged in the surrounding skin and muscle. "God in Heaven," I murmured.

Grabbing my arm with a surprising amount of strength for the pain I imagined he was in, Holmes pleaded with me. "Do . . . whatever . . . you can."

"I . . . I'm not sure what that is," I said, my eyes falling on the bloody smears he spread on my coat sleeve. I closed my eyes and said, "Let me think," knowing there were only seconds in which I could do so.

Snapping my eyes open, I made a decision. Every instinct in me said that if something wasn't done immediately, Holmes would lose the entire limb. I scrambled for my fallen doctor's bag and set it next to me. First, I drew a bottle of alcohol from within and cleansed my hands with it. Then, I found a long section of gauze, medical tape, and a metal instrument used to withdraw rubbish from wounds. I hated to use this on Holmes, but as I sanitized it, too, with the alcohol, I knew I had no choice.

"Holmes, I'm sorry, I'm so sorry to make your pain greater, but stay with me. You're very badly injured and I'm afraid if I don't do something now to sanitize the wound and stop the bleeding, you may very well lose the entire limb."

"Lose . . . ? No, I can't," Holmes said, the strength of his disagreement shining through the agony.

"You won't," I promised, though I shouldn't have sworn any such thing. Despite everything I could do, we were still on a dirty dock instead of a hospital, and I had very limited supplies. The alcohol alone was almost gone and I only had about two yards of gauze and even less tape. Yet I continued with my reassurances. "Holmes, you won't. But I'm afraid I have to use these and pull pieces of bullet and bone from your leg. It's going to be . . . extremely painful. I'm so sorry, Holmes."

"No. Do it. If it needs to be done, do it." A wave of nausea overcame him and he half-turned away from me and began dry heaving. I kept my hand on his knee and the other fisted, on his side, a flimsy attempt to keep his leg immobile. Finally, he collapsed and lay still. I hoped he'd passed out from the pain and I began working. But when I removed the first bit of bullet from his muscle, he screamed. I nearly dropped my instrument in shock. Frozen, I stared at him, unsure I would be able to continue.

Seeming to sense my hesitance, he worked to control his breathing, gripped the front of my shirt, and said, "No, Watson! Continue! You must . . . continue. Please, keep going. It doesn't . . . matter . . . how much pain . . . I'm in."

And so it went. I worked as quickly and skilfully as I was able, but it still brought scream after anguished scream from Holmes. Yet he begged me to continue, so on I went, removing as many bone and bullet fragments as I was able. I did the best I could, but in the end, irrevocable damage was done to the surrounding muscle.

Just when I feared I'd have to leave Holmes to fetch help, a lone policeman came down the dock. He gave us much needed assistance and Holmes was brought to a hospital, where he remained in a coma for several days. When he woke up, he asked to see me.

I entered his room and was met with quite a strange sight, for one so used to seeing Holmes up and about. He was stretched out on the bed wearing a rumpled nightdress, with a blanket covering his lower half, including the cast that went from shin to hip in the hopes of holding his thigh bone in place.

Pulling up a chair next to the bed, I said, "You wished to see me, Holmes?"

"Yes. I was hoping you could tell me when I will be released from this madhouse. I have no patience for nurses continually coming in, disturbing my sleep, or insisting they help me with something supposedly as simple as urinating."

I held back a smile as I responded, "Well, it would prevent stains on your sheets."

I was met with a withering glance. "If I thought for a moment that you were making a joke at my expense, I'd challenge you to a fencing match when I'm back on my feet."

I knew that he expected me to smile and back down, as both of us knew that compared to him, I was less than a rank amateur, barely knowing which end of the sword the handle was on. But today that reference only depressed me.

Holmes noted the crestfallen expression descend over my features and his brow creased. "There's something I don't know about this injury," he said as definitely as if he were the doctor.

Knowing there was no point in denial, I nodded.

"How severe was the damage? When you told me of the situation, I had you operate immediately to prevent loss of the limb. Was my decision wrong?"

"No, no. Not at all. With all my medical knowledge, I can confidently say you made the best possible choice. If I'd thought there was any chance of waiting until you reached a hospital, I would never have subjected you to the pain I know you endured."

"Then something unexpected happened."

"Not entirely . . ."

"Please, just tell me what happened," he requested.

I sighed. "Part of the reason there was so much pain is because the bullet did not pass through cleanly. It shattered part of your femur and fragments of bone lodged themselves into the surrounding muscle." I took a moment to stare at my friend, see if he'd picked up my implied meaning. Yet for someone who could make the strangest connections over the most minute details, he seemed unwilling to make this one.

"Holmes, the muscle damage is irreparable. It's not severe enough to hamper your full ability to walk, but as far as I can estimate, you will need a cane for the rest of your days because your leg will no longer be able to bear your full weight."

Holmes closed his eyes and leaned back so that his head sunk low into the pillow. "A cane. Is there more?"

"There may be a chance you will experience . . . chronic pain. The severity of which we won't know until you're out of the cast, but--"

He held up his hand to stop me. "I need time. I'd like to be alone. I need time to digest this information."

Nothing worried me more than Holmes alone with his thoughts, but seeing as how he had so little control over everything else right now, I could at least grant him the peace of solitude.

The rest of November and all of December passed rather uneventfully. Holmes was able to come back to Baker Street just before Christmas, but except for mindless thank-yous when he received the assistance he needed to get into his bed there, he was quiet. I cannot even begin to describe the depths to which that frightened me. I worried Holmes may have lost his mind, being cooped up away from challenging cases, wondering if LeStrade was solving them or simply catching penny-chasing thieves.

But on the third of January, Holmes's leg was doing remarkably well, and we were able to remove the cast. He was lucid throughout. As he watched the cast being taken off, he listened while I told him how to build up strength in his leg before using it. He barely commented when I told him I planned to temporarily move back into the Baker Street apartment to assist with his therapy.

It wasn't until after I'd helped Holmes through a physical therapy session that he spoke of his fate.

"I've been thinking things over after what you've told me and have come to the obvious conclusion. I'm to live out this life as a cripple."

"Holmes . . ."

"Don't attempt to give me fraudulent sympathies. I'll no longer be looked at as a detective and I'd appreciate your honesty right now more than anything else."

Sighing, I debated the kindest way to give the

honesty he desired. "I cannot, as usual, fault your reasoning. You will, for the rest of your days, need a cane, as I mentioned before. I've already arranged for one to be sent here, because even though physical therapy can do much, it cannot give you back full use of your leg. There was just too much damage." I paused, then tried to throw a brief bit of humour into the conversation. "Of course, your situation could be worse. Do you remember Jonathan Small?"

A tight grin formed on his lips. "He had a wooden leg. Yes, I suppose it is a fortunate thing that amputation was possible to avoid." He stared at me. "Thank you for the cane, John."

At that moment I knew Holmes was shaken to his very core. He never used my first name. It told me how utterly vulnerable he felt in the face of such a grim diagnosis. "Y-you're welcome, Sherlock."

"My decision is final," he said after a brief pause.

"Decision?"

"Yes, it's something I've been thinking about for a month or more. It's been a pestering seed inside my head. If I can no longer . . ." He sighed heavily. "I have no choice. Sherlock Holmes is officially retired."

"Retire? You? Now? But Holmes, surely you can still find the clues, figure out the puzzles, while--"

"While what? That mindless half-wit LeStrade, or worse yet, Inspector Jones, lays all the traps, makes all the arrests, and takes all the credit?" Holmes interrupted. "I can respect them as inspectors; they worked hard to get where they are. But I refuse to respect them as men, for they have no conscience where credit is truly due, especially LeStrade, who would rather have the public believe I'd disappeared."

"Wouldn't you be playing right into his hands if that's what he wants people to think?" However, I seriously doubted it. Holmes was not one to make a decision like this lightly, nor was he one to have an illogical basis for his thoughts and deductions.

"Watson, surely you know me better than that," he admonished. "LeStrade always falls back on me, whether he realizes it or not. Without me there, he'll have to stand on his own, having no one else to blame for the blunders he makes."

I could not fault his reasoning, as usual, but the idea of his retirement depressed me in ways I didn't know possible. Doctors truly are arrogant people, all of us. We always assume that once we save someone's life, they'll be forever grateful. They'll thank us. They'll be in our debt. We never expect to see the shadows of blame around their eyes. The permanent scar of accusation within their glance. I expected to see it from Holmes. I almost welcomed it. Yet he never showed it. Even after he told me of his decision to retire from what he loved doing above everything else in this world, (except perhaps experimenting with his chemistry set,) he never even hinted at blame towards me. While that should have taken the edge off of the guilt I felt, somehow when I was kept up at night by the thoughts that plague us all, my mind would turn to Holmes, and I would feel even worse that he assigned me no blame.

Was this truly the same man who, on so many occasions, told me that deductions flowed through his veins?

Approximately two weeks after his announcement of retirement, Holmes's therapy had progressed well enough that he could, for short periods, walk with the cane I'd ordered for him. Around eleven the next morning, Mrs. Hudson knocked gently on the door. I answered and she handed me the mail, whispering, "Urgent letter for Mr. Holmes."

"I'll see that he gets it at once," I assured.

She tipped her head in thanks and went back downstairs.

I turned slowly as I read the return address. *'From Paris,'* I thought. *'Interesting...'*

"Watson, was that Mrs. Hudson at the door?" Holmes called from his room.

I approached his room and saw him sitting in his wheelchair, a blanket over his lower half, working with his impressive and extensive chemistry set. "Yes, it was. She delivered this letter. Urgent business, she--"

"Yes, yes, I heard her. Why did she not hand it directly to me?"

"I'd wager her to still be a trifle frightened of your temper."

"Hm, yes, very true. I have been something of a beast lately, haven't I?"

"Something of," I murmured in agreement, though his had been a rhetorical statement.

"What does the letter speak of?" he asked abruptly, wheeling himself back from the table. "Would you be so kind as to read it to me?"

"Of course." I took the letter from the envelope and, once it was unfolded, began to recite:

Dear Mr. Holmes,

I implore you, sir, for my need of the detective skills you possess is great. My partner and I now own the grandest opera house in France, the Opera Populaire. But we've had to close down for at least six months, perhaps more! because our central chandelier crashed down, just as the Phantom assured us it would.

Yes, monsieur, the Phantom. That is the reason I'm in need of your expertise. This madman has seized control of the opera house, demanding payments, the best Box seat, and control of casting. Because of these demands, the great diva, La Carlotta, is refusing to perform!

I beg thee, Monsieur Holmes, come to Paris and solve this mystery so that we may revive the opera house and return it to its former glory before this ghost descended in our midst.

His signature, one Jean Andre, was at the bottom. "Curious. What do you make of it, Holmes?"

"That the word 'retirement' has not yet reached French ears."

"But surely you think this is worth looking into!" I exclaimed.

"Hardly. Watson, allow me to see the parchment on which he wrote." His fingertips had barely made contact when he said, "Aha, just as I expected. Do you actually not see, my good man?"

"You know any powers of observation I possess are no match for your trained eye."

"Very well. Several spots over the letter have ink blotches, indicating a lack of patience to release the words from brain to pen. Then consider his use of the words 'beg' and 'implore.' He's a desperate man who doesn't want his riches wasted on a useless endeavour, should patrons of the opera not return after what appears to be so great a calamity. A chandelier crashing down, horrid.

"Then, of course, there's the grade of paper he uses. He is the manager of a successful opera house. Or, once successful, anyway. Yet he uses an incredibly cheap brand of paper to write to me. He is not someone easily parted with his earnings. Probably part of the reason he mentions this 'Phantom' demanding payments.

"Add to that, one can easily surmise from his mention of this 'ghost,' as well as the diva, that he is an easily controlled man, not very dominant at all."

"Brilliant reasoning, as usual. But aren't those exactly the reasons we *should* help these men?"

Holmes did not answer. Instead, he resumed his activities with his chemicals.

Yet in the coming fortnight, I saw a distinct change come over Holmes. He began to walk about with his cane more often, to further exercise what muscles he could in his leg, and he became near obsessed with finding any information possible about this Phantom and the opera house he was said to inhabit. One night, undoubtedly exhausted after a day's excursions, he had retired to his wheelchair and rolled into my room.

"Watson, do you know that the chorus girls in this opera house believe it to be haunted by an actual ghost? Even the ballet instructor is rumoured to have warned others not to speak ill of this 'Phantom.'"

"Indeed?" said I. The perfect logistician, I could tell all this talk of phantoms perplexed and annoyed

Holmes. He was coming closer and closer to declaring his need to find the human responsible.

"That instructor, one Madame Giry, has courteously agreed to speak with me. Since the event Andre mentioned in his letter, everyone has been released from any obligations to the Populaire, and she is using that fact to her advantage. She'll be here the day after tomorrow."

"Would you be offended if I were here as well?" I asked.

"Of course not! You needn't even ask such a question. After the cases we've seen together, I wouldn't dare refuse you now! We're a team, Watson."

Flattered to hear him say that once again, I cheerfully acquiesced and looked forward to speaking with this woman.

As promised, Madame Giry arrived at our door at eleven sharp. She wore a simple black garment that hung to her ankles, and had with her a long black cane. Her silvery brown hair was pulled back and tightly wound into a braided bun, bound at the nape of her neck. I met her at the door and introduced myself, then brought her over to the couch where Holmes was sitting. His cane rested against the back of the couch.

"I'm sorry for not greeting you at the door myself," he said, gesturing for her to take a seat.

"It is all right, Monsieur Holmes, you mentioned your affliction in your telegram," she replied, her French accent prominent in her speech.

"Yes, well," he said, wincing slightly, "please, make yourself comfortable. I notice you have a cane as well. Might I ask what significance yours holds?"

"It is ornamental and nothing more. I use it to help count the beats in music so my dancers are not off on their timing," she explained, thumping the cane on the floor a few times in example.

"Perfectly understandable," Holmes said. "I play the violin, so I know the value of a metronome to keep time."

She nodded, obviously pleased. "Now, Monsieur, you say you want information about the Phantom."

"Yes, I must admit this whole business about a Phantom has left me quite baffled and curious. At first, I wasn't willing to take the case, considering this affliction, as you put it. But there are too many puzzling elements.

For one, why would men of such professional stature believe in this supposed apparition?"

"It is not merely superstitious belief in a ghost, sir. The strange happenings fuelled the fires of gossip and the fallen chandelier finalized their beliefs."

Holmes gave a sardonic smile. "I was being rhetorical, my good lady. But nevertheless, you raise a valid point. The fallen chandelier. But that was undoubtedly the work of a mortal man, not a ghost. Yet somehow I believe this Phantom is considered both. These elements and more are why I had such an interest in speaking with you. Madame Giry, I have done research into your background and from that research, have concluded that of all who are employed by the Opera Populaire, you are most likely to have personal knowledge of the Phantom, more so than being privy to the rumours and stories of dancers and chorus girls. I believe you have a basis of fact to go off of where this Phantom is concerned."

Her eyes widened slightly and her straight back hunched forward as she leaned in, seemingly about to give us a great secret. "You are correct, monsieur. Years ago, when I was just a girl, my mother took me to a gypsy carnival. Their main attraction was a boy they called the 'Skeleton Face.' He was horribly deformed, but had the voice of an angel. The carnival's owner, a cruel man named Gustavo, forced the boy to sing for the crowd, or to throw his voice to make it seem like one of the great beasts in its cage was talking. At the end of the act, Gustavo forced the boy to remove the sack he kept over his head and always, always several ladies in the crowd would faint from the shock of seeing his ruined form."

Holmes leaned forward, interested. "And you believe this boy to have become the Phantom?"

"I can only suspect. You see, he escaped the carnival shortly after the day I saw him. Strangled the owner to do it, or so the stories say. I cannot blame him, for there was no crueller man than Gustavo. He made that poor boy stand up there without any shield for his face, even as the men threw rotting fruit at him."

"Intriguing . . . And he escaped and began to terrorize the opera house?"

"Oh, no, Monsieur Holmes, the opera house was not built yet. I don't know where he was in the interim. Many years later, twenty perhaps, or more, a man named Charles Garnier set about to take control of the construction of the Opera Populaire. No one could imagine him having such beautiful plans in mind, but he'd drawn them up and showed anyone who challenged him why they were superior. Yet his passion and drive seemed to be coming from an outside source."

"You mean to tell me that this deformed child -- now a man-- was an architect as well?"

She nodded and cleared her throat. "May I have some water?"

Holmes nodded at me and I arose dutifully to fulfil her wish. When she'd taken several sips, she continued. "When it was completed, there was no finer building than the Opera Populaire. But from the first day I set foot inside, it felt as if a presence lingered. A somewhat malevolent one. And it wasn't long before the chorus girls started their rumours of a shadow here, missing hairpieces there. Soon, instead of blaming one another, stories of the opera ghost began to circulate among them. It wasn't long before anything that went wrong or missing was blamed on him."

"The petty jealousies of dancers and singers mixed with fear caused their imaginations to conjure an opera ghost."

"So it would seem, to an outsider. But the opera ghost is not just a figment of overactive imaginations. Soon, more respected people began seeing what they swore was a black cape swirling around a dark corner. However, this 'opera ghost' was quite harmless. I believe he enjoyed the rumours. Got a rise out of scaring the girls. Yes, things could have stayed the way they were, simple rumours flowing through the corridors, had the new managers not defied him when they started receiving the notes."

"Notes?" I asked, speaking for the first time.

She nodded at me. "Yes, the Phantom wrote them to tell the management of his demands."

"Do you have any of these notes, or recall what any of them said?" Holmes asked.

"I was only ever able to salvage one, monsieur. The very first one that he wrote to the first manager of the Populaire." She reached into a fold of her dress and brought out the yellowed parchment to hand to Holmes. He read it, then handed it to me and asked, "What do you make of it, Watson?"

Knowing that he just wanted me to admit his superior observational skills again, but unable to resist the challenge, I read the words scrawled over the parchment.

Welcome to my opera house. Considering the success of the Populaire in the past year, I request my rightful payment. Twenty thousand francs a month, to be delivered by Mme Giry to Box five on the first Sunday of each month, eight 'o clock sharp. I've been over the books and know that this is but a pittance of the sum you bring in. Therefore, I do not foresee any problems with your acquiescence.

Also, I have grown accustomed to quality seating in places such as this, so you will leave Box five empty during each performance. Dire consequences shall befall you should you ignore these requests.

"Interesting that he refers to it as *his* opera house," I commented softly.

"I thought the same. Whoever wrote that note must

also have been the driving force behind Garnier." Holmes took back the note and glanced at it. "His mention of the books means that he has access to the offices in the opera house as well." He looked again at Madame Giry, returning the note to her. "What else can you tell us?"

"Well, the manager was a very superstitious sort, always crossing himself, or throwing salt over his shoulder, so he took this note very seriously. Each first Sunday, I took an envelope containing the twenty thousand francs up to Box five and set it on the velvet cushion of the lone chair. The second time and each time after, there was always something left behind for me. Sometimes it was money, but always some kind of gift."

"The Phantom was rewarding you," Holmes said slowly.

"I'm quite sure. And it would have gone on this way, quite pleasantly, but then Carlotta came to us."

"The diva."

"Yes." An ugly look crossed Madame Giry's face. "She came to us from Spain and a more conceited creature never existed. She began placing demands on the manager immediately for a bigger dressing room, more pay, more quality dancers or chorus singers. She even insisted that she would not perform if someone was declared her understudy!" The woman paused, obviously frustrated, to take another long sip of water. "I'm sorry, gentlemen, but my dislike of this woman is great."

"Not a problem, I assure you. However, could we move to more present times? I'm sure that Carlotta came to you some ten or eleven years ago, as I recall hearing about a rising Spanish star in the world of opera some time ago."

"Yes, monsieur. It was about eleven years ago. Her demands increased over the years until finally, it seemed nothing anyone could do would please her. She grated on the manager's last nerve until, for health reasons, he decided to retire. Even with the Phantom's monthly salary, he'd made more than he ever dreamed of while running the Populaire. He brought in messieurs Andre and Firmin to take over, telling them of the Phantom's allowance and the foolishness of attempting to sell Box five to the public. Yet even after the note messieurs Andre and Firmin received from the Phantom, they felt it was a joke."

"They weren't as superstitious, I take it?"

"Not at all. They couldn't fathom why their

predecessor had indulged the Phantom. Box five was a quality box, they said, and they could catch a handsome price for it. There wasn't a reasonable cause to not sell it. But then, during a rehearsal, a set piece almost hit Carlotta and she ran off, refusing to perform that night. The managers were beside themselves. They didn't know what to do since Carlotta had no understudy and I'm sure the idea of refunding a full house made them feel faint. But then my daughter Meg suggested Christine Daae sing the lead."

"Daae . . . I feel as though I've heard that name before," Holmes murmured.

"You may have heard of her father. He was an excellent violinist from Sweden."

"Yes, of course. I recall studying his bowing for a time when I first began to play myself. I'm sorry, do go on. This Christine, was she a success?"

"Oh, yes, sir. She was amazing and brought the house down on opening night. Everyone said so. But then she disappeared for several days. And when Carlotta came back, her status as a diva, as well as the benefits, were returned to her."

"Disappeared, you say? What happened to her?"

"Well, the night she sang Carlotta's part, her childhood friend, Raoul, came to see the opera. They met in Christine's dressing room, but she rebuffed his attempts to get her to join him for dinner. He paid no heed, however, and left her dressing room to bring his carriage around to a closer entrance. When he tried to enter her room again, he found the door locked and heard a man's voice within, beckoning Christine."

"The Phantom," I asserted.

"Yes. He took her, but not out of cruelty. I believe he wanted to reward her for her triumph that night. However, the managers took it as proof of her unreliability, completely ignoring the letters they received, praising her, and the standing ovation that greeted her performance.

"The Phantom told them that in the next production, *Il Muto,* I believe it was, Christine was to play the countess and Carlotta was to be placed in the silent role of the pageboy. He would watch the performance in his normal seat and if they ignored him, they would face dire consequences."

"Considering the chandelier, I think it's fair to say the Phantom was ignored," Holmes muttered.

"You are correct, he was denied, but the chandelier came later that night. Carlotta portrayed the countess, and in the course of the performance, the Phantom made himself known. It disturbed the scene and the audience quite a bit, but everyone onstage can at least pass themselves off as a professional and knows how to carry a show. They began the scene again but this time, Carlotta's voice gave out, making horrible croaking noises whenever she tried to sing. She ran off, and the managers said the show would continue in ten minutes when Christine would play the countess.

"Before she came out, though, Joseph Buquet's body fell from one of the rafters, hanging there in the middle of the stage for all to see."

"The Phantom murdered him," Holmes said, his eyebrows going up.

"Yes, though I don't believe it was connected to his displeasure over the casting."

"And who was this Joseph Buquet?" Holmes asked.

"He was a dirty-minded stagehand who could never keep to himself. He enjoyed feeding the flames of the Opera Ghost mystery and could quite often be found ignoring his work and instead, telling tales about the Phantom to purposely frighten the girls."

Holmes sat back and adjusted his leg to make himself more comfortable. "This is an interesting web so far. But tell me, Madame Giry, this Phantom, 'Skeleton Face,' Opera Ghost . . . Does he have an actual name?"

She looked at Holmes in absolute amazement. "You are the first person to ever ask what his name is, Monsieur Holmes. No one else has ever cared . . ."

"Well, it's a matter of some importance, I think. He is not some spectre, he is a living, breathing man, and he must have been christened with a name."

"Yes, sir, he was. His name is Erik, sir."

"Erik. Good. You said it was the same night as this *Il Muto* production that the chandelier crashed down, but later on?"

"Yes, that's right. It must have been about three quarters of an hour after Buquet's body was discovered. From inside the theatre, we heard maniacal laughter and then his voice yelling 'go!' Then the chandelier began to rock dangerously back and forth and crashed down in the orchestra pit and the middle of the stage."

"That must have been an incredible tragedy," I

said. "I can only imagine the ruin an event like that would cause. The managers should feel fortunate to assume they can re-open in as little as six months."

"Thankfully, there were very few casualties. Most of the orchestra had left their instruments and gotten out the door under the stage and all of the dancers and singers had fled when Buquet fell from the rafters. There were a few instrumentalists we lost and several people were injured in the chaotic rush to leave the opera house." She continued somewhat bitterly. "Of course, the main concern for the managers is replacing all the instruments."

"Indeed," Holmes said, his eyebrows going up again. "I eagerly anticipate the version of these events I'll get from messieurs Andre and Firmin."

"Does that mean you're coming to Paris, Monsieur Holmes?" Madame Giry asked.

"Yes. I believe I already mentioned I was taking this case. If not, though, rest assured, Watson and I shall leave in a few days' time. Tell me, repairs are taking place at the opera, but what of the managers, the cast, the stagehands?"

"Most of us have gratefully taken this time off. However, the managers are constantly there, overseeing the reconstruction. More prominent members of the cast still come by the opera, though no one has seen Carlotta since she ran off the stage. Monsieur Firmin insists that the opera house will be fully restored within two and a half months time, though."

"Two and a half months? That would mean that three and a half have already passed since the chandelier's destruction?"

"Yes."

"Watson, when was the manager's letter sent?"

I found it on his chemistry table. "The letter appears to be dated the beginning of November," I said.

"The post isn't usually that slow. I wonder why it took so long to get to you," Mme Giry said.

"Perhaps the managers delayed sending it to me, unsure of what, if anything, I could truly do. No matter. Two and a half months, you say. Is there any significance to that time frame?"

"Of course, sir. The annual masquerade ball. Everyone in Paris wishes to attend one, but invitations are extended only to opera house members and some of the more elite members of French society. It is a grand night, full of costumes and drink, dancing and merriment--"

For once, I'm sure I observed something another's casual glance would miss. Holmes's eyes lit up at Madame Giry's description of the ball, but just as quickly, they flickered to his leg and lost their joy. "It sounds delightful, my good woman, but I'm afraid my time grows short. I'm sorry to interrupt, but if I'm to get to Paris, arrangements must be made."

"Oh, yes. Excuse me. I do tend to ramble, don't I?" She stood up, handing me the glass, now empty. "I look forward to seeing you in Paris, gentlemen. I'll show myself out."

After she'd gone, I looked at Holmes. "What do you make of this business, Holmes?"

"She certainly is a spirited woman. This Phantom . . . Erik, rather, is nothing but a man. Yet he is determined to terrorize those around him in such a manner that he seems a spectre." Holmes cradled his chin with his hand. "I wonder what his motivation is."

"What do you mean?" I asked him.

He met my eyes. "Even if this man is crazy, he must have a reason behind his actions. Insanity is never acknowledged by the sufferer and therefore their actions are even more calculated than a normal person's, following a distinct pattern of meticulousness."

"Couldn't that Miss Daae be the Phantom's connection, or reason, as you put it?"

"Ah, the young singer. Yes, she is a possibility. But really, Watson, a woman being a man's entire motivation behind such acts?"

"What if he was in love with her?"

Holmes let out a short, sarcastic laugh. "Watson, you do not truly believe something so absurd, do you?"

Considering that I had quite a happy marriage with my wife, I felt inclined to speak on love's behalf. "Truly believe in love? Yes, I can quite confidently say I most assuredly believe in that."

Holmes sensed my indignation. "Watson, I was not trying to imply anything concerning you or your wife."

"Holmes, may I speak frankly?"

"Of course. You needn't ask."

"Just because you don't believe in a concept does not mean it's not something very real and a driving factor for others."

My friend gave a sardonic smile and I couldn't help bracing myself for his berating. Instead, his face fell and all he would say was, "I'll have more definite facts once I speak with her." He levelled his gaze on me. "You are certain you wish to accompany me?"

"Yes, by all means. I'm curious in more than one way."

"Really? Please enlighten me."

"Well, how could a man survive the way that he has?"

"And what way is that, Watson?"

"I-- Well, he must have--" I stopped, not sure how to continue.

Holmes held up his index finger. "Precisely. We shall go to Paris and find this Phantom. Only then can we learn any facts to give us anything by which to theorize. Though you could not answer, you bring up an interesting point. If this man has such a horrid face, he can't very well live openly in French society."

"How do we find out where he has been living?"

"The opera house is our key. I find him within those walls and I reason with him. If I cannot reason with him, we can at least bring him to justice."

"Do you think the police can handle him?"

Holmes gave me a sardonic smile. "Watson, do not be ridiculous. I said nothing of the police."

From the Journal of John H. Watson, M.D.

When Holmes and I arrived in Paris, we checked into a very pleasant-looking hotel and then caught a carriage to the Populaire. We walked into the manager's office to come face-to-face with messieurs Andre and Firmin. When the men noticed us, they came over and gratefully grasped Holmes's free hand. It was several minutes before either of them noticed the silver-headed cane and realized exactly how much Holmes used it to assist his balance.

"Monsieur Holmes," Firmin said, staring at the cane, "we were given to understand that you were, among other things, a master fencer. Pray tell us, is this some kind of clever disguise?"

The anguished expression that crossed Sherlock Holmes's eyes nearly caused me physical pain. He closed his eyes for a long moment and I noticed his fingers turning white at the knuckle as they gripped his cane more tightly.

"No, I don't mean to disappoint you, gentlemen, but this cane is a needed accessory. I suffered an accident a short time ago that greatly affected the muscles in my right thigh. But I assure you, though my skills in mobility have decreased, my detection skills have not been diminished in the least."

Andre sighed and glanced at Firmin. In a hushed voice, he said, "I had no idea I'd acquired the services of a cripple."

Holmes's eyes hardened and the cords in his neck stood out prominently as they tightened. "Excuse me, but there is nothing faulty about my hearing."

At least they both had the decency to look embarrassed.

"I'm sorry, Monsieur Holmes, but you must understand our position," Andre said. "This phantom at first was nothing more than chorus girl superstition. But now he is this awesome spectre, seemingly capable of flight from one balcony to the next! With one so nimble as he, how can you hope to catch him?"

"Well, gentlemen, I assure you, even in my finest days, I could not jump from one balcony to the next. After studying some of the structural points of the opera house, I can conclude they are at least seventy feet apart from one another. I will not chase your Phantom, but I will find out who he is and where he's hiding. Now, I've done some reading about the opera house and its history, but I'd like you to fill me in on what exactly the Phantom has done here. When did he first begin showing himself?"

"He has never shown himself," Firmin answered. "Oh, chorus girls claim to have seen a man in black whisking about on the catwalks, but that's no more than powder room drama."

"Are you quite sure of that?" Holmes asked. "Tell me about all the incidents that led up to the crashing of the great chandelier you mentioned in your letter."

Again, the men glanced at one another. "It began with Christine Daae," Andre said.

"She was a chorus girl," Firmin continued. "It was just after we took over management. A rehearsal for *Hannibal* was going on, but then our diva, La Carlotta, had a near-accident with one of the set pieces and refused to sing. We suddenly had no star, and it was the first performance we were overseeing! It was a full house and we would have been ruined had we refunded everyone's money! Then a dancer suggested one of the chorus girls, one Christine Daae, to sing Carlotta's part. It turned out she has a very pleasant voice, and in many ways, she saved us. But she's a complete unknown and people come to hear the great divas. So when Carlotta came back to us, we decided to put Miss Daae back in the chorus."

"I'll wager our resident Phantom wasn't fond of your decision," Holmes commented softly. He gestured to one of the two chairs in front of the managers' desk. "May I sit down?"

"Yes, yes, of course," Firmin answered. Holmes sat down as Firmin continued. "And you are correct. The Phantom apparently had ideas of Miss Daae being our new diva."

"Was this Christine Daae a success?" I asked.

"Well, yes. Though even if we wanted to have her as our new diva, she is not particularly reliable. After the performance where she starred in Carlotta's role, she disappeared for several days. No one saw her or heard from her and then she reappeared just after Carlotta came back to us. So you see why we didn't follow these instructions," Firmin said, opening a drawer and handing Holmes a piece of parchment, the broken wax seal still present. It was red wax, in the shape of a skull.

I peeked over Holmes's shoulder as his eyes grazed the note. Written in red ink, undoubtedly to simulate blood, it read simply that the managers had received several other notes detailing how his theatre was to be run, but they'd paid no heed to the instructions. It went on to say that he'd returned Christine Daae to them and was insistent that her career progress. Therefore, in the new production of the opera *Il Muto,* Christine was to be cast as the countess, and Carlotta was to play the pageboy, a silent role.

The entire letter had a rather charming, amiable nature to it, except for the last two lines, which simply stated, *"I shall watch the performance from my normal seat in Box 5, which will be kept empty for me. Should these commands be ignored, a disaster beyond your imagination will occur."*

"Interesting," Holmes murmured. "And where are these other notes that are mentioned?"

"Well, to be honest, we didn't keep any of them. No one thought they were truly any threat."

"By no one, I'm sure you mean the two of you," Holmes said with a measure of sarcasm.

"Would *you* believe any of these notes to be an honest threat?" Andre asked, levelling a look of disgust at Holmes and me. I felt rather indignant at being included, considering I'd been silent throughout this exchange.

"I can't judge that, now can I, since you saw no reason to keep them," Holmes told them, meeting their gaze.

There was a tense and furious stare-down before Andre turned away from Holmes and asked, "Shall we continue?"

"Yes, please."

Firmin gripped the edge of the desk. "We assigned the roles as we saw fit, with Miss Daae in the silent role. Halfway through the production, however, the Phantom's voice resounded through the theatre, demanding his instructions be followed about leaving Box five vacant. Christine let out an exclamation that it was the Phantom, and Carlotta berated her. We began the scene over, but several lines in, Carlotta's throat began letting out these horrible noises. She couldn't control it at all and in the middle of that, the Phantom started laughing, then suddenly shouted, 'Behold! She is singing to bring down the chandelier!' Carlotta ran off in an understandably hysterical state and I took centre stage to try and stop the mounting panic. I announced that the show would continue in ten minutes time, with Christine Daae in the role of countess. While costume changes took place, they could be entertained by the ballet from Act three."

"During the ballet," Andre added, "the body of Joseph Buquet fell from one of the rafters and hung for all to see in the middle of the stage! The Phantom murdered him and is determined to ruin us! How else would you explain showing a dead body on the stage after we didn't follow his cockamamie instructions?"

Holmes's eyes widened. "You see a murder as nothing more than an attempt to ruin you?"

Both managers opened their mouths, then thinking better of Holmes's question, remained quiet. Holmes stood up and walked to the door. "Gentlemen, I believe I have enough information from you to begin my investigation. I should like to talk to others in the opera house, specifically this Christine Daae and La Carlotta. Please inform them I will call on them within the next few days." He turned away, but turned back a moment later. "I will bill you within the day with my fee."

With that, Holmes opened the door, glanced at me, and walked out leaving the managers standing there with amazed expressions.

I caught up with my friend about ten feet down the

hallway as he headed towards the grand staircase. We left the opera and went back to our room at the hotel where Holmes settled on the bed and I sat at the desk.

"Buffoons! Ignorant imbeciles! I don't hesitate to say that those men deserve the ire of this Phantom!"

"I do admit they didn't seem to be particularly concerned with their staff, but--"

"Oh, it's not just that, Watson. Those foolhardy men would rather have a tone-deaf has-been as their 'diva' when it would obviously benefit them to place Miss Daae in the spotlight. The only reason they haven't, aside from Carlotta's wrath, is because of the request from someone they are ill-at-ease to be obliged to."

"But Holmes, what of the murder? What of the chandelier? If this Phantom did these things, he is obviously not of sound mind."

Holmes stared at me for so long without speaking that I squirmed in my seat. "I draw no conclusions about Erik. I have no facts about him yet. Just hearsay from Madame Giry and from those two buffoons. Who, by the way, are the only ones I'm convinced are not of sound mind."

"What is your plan, then?"

"We shall rest tonight. I'm sufficiently agitated right now that any investigation would be hindered enormously, and in a place as big as the Opera Populaire, I do not wish to be hindered. Something tells me I do not have much time to find this Phantom and reason with him."

"Indeed? And why is that, Holmes?" I asked as I reached for my doctor's bag. I'd noticed Holmes was starting to massage his leg, something he did when he was either extremely annoyed, or his leg was in sufficient pain. I guessed it was a combination of the two and wanted to give him something to numb the sting.

"From what I've gathered so far from our ever-so-helpful ballet instructor and those idiot managers, plus the history I read of the Populaire, Erik has had a decade and a half, at least, to act. Why now? Why now make his appearance so obvious a thing?"

"Well, the managers we met with are new," I reasoned. "They are the ones not following his instructions--"

"Yes, but that's nothing more than a piece of the puzzle. Erik has cornerstones, four to be specific, that are guiding his actions. I'm certain Miss Daae is one, as is La

Carlotta's fall from success. The other two, I can only speculate on right now and I dare not speak of those guesses. I wish for certainty." He noticed the small bottle I'd finally retrieved from my bag. "Oh, is that one of your marvellous sedatives? I'm afraid my leg is being a frightful bother."

"I noticed you were pressing your knuckles to your thigh. This should alleviate the pain and help you sleep," I said as I mixed several drops from the bottle into a glass of water I hastily fetched. He took a quick sip and wiped his lips after I handed it to him. When he gave me the empty glass some fifteen minutes later, he looked somewhat more relaxed.

"Thank you, Watson. I believe I'll sleep peacefully now. When we rise tomorrow, we immediately seek out Christine Daae and speak to her."

I nodded my agreement and then watched out of the corner of my eye as he drifted to sleep, still in the clothes and coat he wore when we arrived. Letting out a small sigh, I allowed my mind to wander while I jotted down notes and details of conversations about this mysterious case. Of course I'd seen Holmes cautious about cases before; never did he just blindly charge in without first deducing and knowing every bit of information he could. But I'd never, in all my years at his side, seen him hesitate as he had today.

Of course, one had to suppose that his uncertainty could be a ruse. However, I thought better. He did not have his complete physical fortitude, as he was continually reminded, and that could make any man shudder. Holmes had something to prove. Not to others. Others, myself included, I feared, be damned. He was out to prove it to himself. God save the world from unsolved mysteries if he failed.

My First Meeting with Christine Daae

"Monsieur Holmes," a young woman cried as she ran up to me. "Monsieur Holmes, I must speak with you."

I turned slowly to face her, fingering my pipe as it hung from my lips.

"Monsieur Holmes," she said breathlessly as she stopped in front of me. "Please tell me something. I must know!"

"Yes, my dear?"

"Do you truly intend to bring Er-- this opera ghost to justice?"

"That is my ultimate intent. Though what justice means for a being such as he, I cannot say."

"You do not mean to turn him over to the police, then?"

I let out a short, sarcastic bark of a laugh. "Mademoiselle, if this was something ordinary policemen could handle, I would not have been summoned."

She breathed a sigh of relief. "Please, monsieur, allow me to introduce myself. I am Christine Daae. Messieurs Andre and Firmin said you wished to speak with me."

"News travels fast around here. How did you recognize me, if I may ask?" I doused my pipe and placed it back in the inner pocket of my coat.

"Monsieur Andre mentioned that you relied on a cane and since you have one and I didn't recognize you, I assumed," she answered.

I felt that familiar squeeze in my chest when she mentioned my cane. Was I now to be known for it instead of my mind? I shook my head, not wanting to contemplate that fate and asked if we could speak somewhere less populated by those with curious ears. There were too many construction workers and stagehands walking in and out of doors into the hallways for my comfort.

"Of course. Let us go into my dressing room."

"Excellent." I followed her and thought about how the day had started. I'd woken feeling marvellously better, my leg barely giving me a twinge of pain. Watson, however, had woken with a chill. I told him to stay out of the cold Paris air and to take care of himself. I could handle speaking with Miss Daae and doing some sleuthing on my own. He sent himself to bed with barely an argument, and I dressed and headed on my way.

Once inside the opera house, I took some time to explore the theatre from the back row. Ladders, wooden poles, and pulleys were everywhere; but I could tell where the chandelier once hung. I followed its obvious route and saw that it would have crashed down centre-stage and, depending on the size of the chandelier, half of it could have easily landed in the vast orchestra pit.

My eyes had scanned the different balcony seats and I noticed one was far closer to the stage than the others. Instinct told me this was the Phantom's box, Box Five. Determined to get a closer look, I asked the first person I found to escort me to the box. He couldn't, but pointed me in the right direction.

Box Five did give me something more than I expected. Fairly large, it had one seat in the middle, about six feet from the edge of the balcony, with black curtains behind it on either side, pulled back with gold cords. Upon investigation of the chair, I noticed a tear of material wedged between the arm and the seat. Black, velvet on one side, satin on the other, it smelled faintly of mildew. The same faint smell I noticed from the letter Madame Giry had handed to me in Baker Street and that I caught whiff of from the one note the managers had kept. Finding that rather interesting, I pocketed the scrap of cloth and decided not to press my luck. If Erik really was someone who could see all corners of the opera house, I didn't want to attract his attention before I was ready.

And that was how, on my way back to the entrance, Christine Daae caught up to me.

We entered her dressing room and the first thing I noticed was that she had an enormous mirror covering almost an entire wall. The mirror was at least eight feet tall and seven feet wide.

"Very impressive mirror, mademoiselle," I commented.

"Thank you, monsieur," she said, giving a small curtsy. "It was rather imposing when I first got this room, but now . . . it's like an old friend." She quickly sat at her vanity and began nervously brushing her hair. Her left ring finger held a very impressive silver band, a rather large sapphire set in the middle.

"That's a lovely ring you have, Miss Daae. Are you engaged?" I asked.

Her reaction confirmed my thoughts. Her back stiffened and she whirled around to face me, at the same time covering the ring with her right hand and staring at the exquisite carpet.

"You know more about Erik than you let on to others, Miss Daae. Would you care to enlighten me as to how much you know?"

Her eyes met mine. "Y-you know his name. How do you know his name?"

I smiled slightly. "I have my sources. Mademoiselle, I was telling you the truth. Erik has no need to fear me. And neither do you." I sat down on a chair a respectable distance from her. "Now, please, tell me what you know."

"Erik . . ." She nervously turned the ring around on her finger, her eyes flitting from it to me. "He gave me this ring. But I cannot keep it! My heart does not belong to him, it belongs to Raoul, the vicomte. Yet . . ." She sighed and turned so pale I was worried she would faint. She was such a slight woman, very thin and barely standing over five feet.

"Please, my dear, calm yourself."

"I'm sorry. This entire ordeal has been so very trying." She turned to face the giant mirror and murmured, "Monsieur Holmes, have you heard the tales of the Angel of Music?"

"No, I'm afraid I haven't."

"Then I'm sure they were just stories my father made up on those stormy days when Raoul and I would watch the waves from the sea. But he assured me the angel was real!" She met my reflection's gaze and continued passionately. "My father said that when he died he would send the Angel of Music. Monsieur, my father is dead and I have heard the Angel!"

"The Phantom," I murmured.

"I'm forced to believe so now. But he was so gentle at first . . . His voice came from this very mirror, dictating and coaching me, bringing my voice to its full potential. His voice is so lovely, so pure, and he spoke to me with such kindness . . . How was I to know that such a monster lay behind that voice?"

"A monster?" I asked, having decided that the less information I volunteered, the better.

"It happened after my first real success here. I had begged Erik to appear to me, so that I could look upon the face of the inspiration behind my voice. He'd become ever so angry and refused to speak with me for several days before the performance. But the night *Hannibal* debuted, I found a rose in my dressing room, hanging from the mirror on my vanity. I knew it was from him and when I took my place onstage, I sang my best to please him."

"And did you please him?"

"Oh, yes, monsieur! I came back to my dressing room and heard his voice. But then my friend Meg, one of the dancers, came and asked me how my voice had improved so. As I described it to her, I also attempted imploring my Angel to show himself to me. When Meg had to leave minutes later, I'd hoped my Angel would appear. Instead, Raoul stepped into my room."

"Now, one thing I'm unclear on. Who is this Raoul? You spoke of the vicomte, so I assume he has something of a title."

"Yes, he does. Raoul, first and foremost, is a dear childhood friend of mine. He lived nearby the cottage that Father and I stayed in and he would come over to hear Father's stories. Once, we were outside and Father warned me I was too close to the sea, but I paid no heed. I was young and wanted to get as close to the waves as I could. I believe the silly, fanciful part of me thought I would be carried off on top of them and rescued by some merman prince." She laughed gently. "My scarf blew off as I stood and it landed in the sea. When I cried out, Raoul ran into the waves without a second thought and rescued my scarf, though he was soaked to the skin.

"But now he is the Vicomte De Chagny, he should not be seen with a chorus girl. And the Angel of Music demanded vigilance. He did not want me distracted by earthly desires . . ."

"I see," I muttered, taking my pipe back out and turning it over, tracing it with my fingers.

"When Raoul left, the Angel was upset, insisting to know who this boy was, who dared bask in the glory I accomplished that night. I tried to pacify him, to tell him I was his alone, I was remaining attentive only to him. I had turned Raoul away, hadn't I? Even though it broke my heart to do so!

"It seemed to ease his mind and my Angel rewarded me. He was angry when I asked to see his face once again, but then he took me with him to where he lives. It seemed like a wonderful dream at first-- there were candles all around, and there was a lake, and a boat . . . I'm sorry, my memory becomes very fuzzy when I try to recall . . ."

"Do not over exert yourself, but do try. I'm interested in what you remember," I said, leaning forward over my left leg.

"I remember . . . there--there was mist. Mist on a huge, glass-like lake. I already mentioned the abundance of candles and at the edge of the lake was a boat. I must have fainted, because swirling faces covered by white masks haunted my dreams. After that, I recall waking in a beautiful bed with black lace curtains surrounding it. When I got up to explore where I was, I heard the oddest music from an organ. I looked and there was Erik, playing as if he was possessed. I approached him, wondering what face I would discover behind the mask on his face. I was sure then that he truly was an angel descended from Heaven. That his beauty would be too much for me to bear and that was why he covered his face. Two times I attempted to remove the mask, but each time, he seemed about to turn and catch me in the act. On the third, however, I succeeded." Christine stopped talking and two tears slipped down her flushed cheeks.

"His face was not what you expected," I said.

"Oh, monsieur, how can someone with such a beautiful voice have such a ruined face?" she cried passionately. "He has the visage of a monster! And when I removed his mask, he turned on me as one. He screamed at me, accusing me of horrible treachery, and told me I could never be free!

"But then his yelling seemed to almost cause him physical pain, and he collapsed at the foot of the organ, gasping. He clawed at the right side of his face, almost as if he could rid himself of that hideous exterior, at the same time reaching his left hand out to me, for I still held his mask."

"And did you give it back to him?"

"Yes. I handed it back and he immediately took it and replaced it on his face. A calm seemed to settle over him then and he insisted I must get back, for the fools who run his theatre would be missing me."

I chuckled sarcastically. "Considering how they feel about Carlotta, I doubt you were missed. But I do appreciate his acknowledgement that the managers are fools."

"Monsieur Holmes, what will you do about Erik? I know now that he was never a true Angel of Music, even though he has the voice and teaching ability of one, yet . . . I do not wish him to come to any harm."

"Miss Daae, before I endeavour to answer that, tell me what happened the night of *Il Muto.*"

Christine instantly paled again. "That night . . . that night was one horrible mistake after another."

"I could make that deduction from the final outcome. However, I need details. I've heard enough of what happened onstage, but what about when it was declared that you would come back as the countess?"

Sighing, she took a deep breath and said, "After Joseph Buquet's body came down, I wanted to escape. Raoul followed me and I guided him to the roof, assuming it was the one place we'd be safe. I tried to tell him about Erik, about seeing his world, about seeing his *face,* but Raoul would not listen. He insisted it was a horrible dream I'd had. But I know it wasn't! Erik is as real as you or I, though he appears to be a phantom because of the tricks and illusions he uses to keep himself hidden. No one could accept a face such as that."

"Then why do you wear his ring?" I asked.

Once again, her eyes flitted from my eyes to the ring and she nervously twisted it. "I told you, Erik said I can never be free."

"But it's the vicomte's world you wish to live in, is

it not?"

"Oh, monsieur, surely you can understand the love between a man and a woman!"

It appeared Watson had been on to something when he chastised me about not giving love credit enough as a suitable motive, after all. "I can honestly say I have no grasp of it whatsoever. I am a man of logic. Of statistics. Of facts. Love does not, and has not ever, fallen under any of those three categories."

"You have never been in love? I cannot deny that my feelings for Raoul are perhaps childish. But he has promised to protect me. He does care for me. Yet while I am with Erik . . . he has opened up my mind, he's taken my soul to places it only longed to be! Yet I cannot belong with him."

"Mademoiselle, you must not look to me to make this choice for you. If there even is a choice to make. Either this Phantom has your heart, or the Vicomte does. You must say goodbye to one if you do not wish to lose them both."

Perhaps my words were seen as too harsh, for she fell silent for several minutes, refusing to speak. I continued to finger my pipe, wondering if she was too fragile a thing to be pushed this way, when she finally spoke. "Yes, you are a knowledgeable man and I must take your words as heartfelt. I do not believe you wish me to betray either man, and I should not have assumed you did."

"Thank you, mademoiselle. You're correct, one should never assume. It is only when we know facts that logical, rational decisions and judgments can be made."

"While on the rooftop," she continued, "as I said, Raoul tried to convince me that everything was only a dream, a horrible dream. Then . . . then he declared his love for me, and I . . . I reciprocated. And that was when we heard it."

"Heard it?" I asked.

"An anguished scream. From the golden angel statue above us on the roof. He heard me! He heard me betray him!"

"And that's when the maniacal laughter began and he crashed the chandelier down," I murmured. "But simply out of jealousy? It doesn't make sense . . ."

After asking her several more questions about what had transpired that night, I left her to her thoughts. I had much to think about myself and the more I considered this puzzle, the more I wished I could find and speak with the central figure of it all--Erik, the Phantom of the Opera.

Christine's almost accusation concerning my understanding of the love between a man and a woman came to haunt me throughout my ride back to the hotel. Despite what I asserted in front of Watson, I understood the Phantom's position only too well. Far from not believing in love, I had believed in it too much, and for a time, been broken because of it. I had been in the midst of that same tragic and wondrous land, when I was right around her age, but had pushed it out of my mind years ago in favour of logic, facts, cold calculations that didn't have the ability to rip a heart to shreds. At least, not my heart.

When I went back in the door to Watson's and my room, I was in a sufficiently melancholy mood. Watson was still asleep in the second bed so I went to the far corner near the window, lit my pipe, and sat upon the window seat, staring out into the bleak day until the light disappeared and the sky was black.

From the Journal of John H. Watson, M.D.

It was several days before I recovered from the cold that kept me bedridden just after we arrived in Paris. But when I woke up on the fourth morning after our arrival, I found I felt enormously better. I washed, dressed, and was about to go out for breakfast when I saw Holmes sitting by the window, pipe hanging limply from his lips, just staring out at the sky.

"Holmes?" I said as I approached him. "Holmes, are you all right?"

He didn't answer me. It was as if he didn't notice I was standing there. I'd seen Holmes in his melancholy stints before. He warned me of this odd personality quirk before we ever shared a room on Baker Street. But somehow it surprised me that he should have fallen in one while we were here on this case. He'd asserted that we didn't have much time and had to utilize what time we were given as intelligently as possible. However, I knew from experience that next to nothing could pull him from the clutches of such a depression, so with a heavy heart, I left the room for breakfast.

I came back about an hour later to find Holmes still in the same position, though this time, his head faced the door.

"Watson, I've missed you. How are you feeling? When did you get up?" he asked me.

"I've been up for at least three hours now. I'm feeling marvellously better this morning, thank you. You didn't respond to my efforts, so I went out to breakfast, hoping you'd be in better spirits when I returned."

"Better spirits . . . Indeed." Holmes sighed deeply. "Despite this cloud that has descended upon me, I realized while you were gone that I couldn't let it deter me from my task. Where is my cane?"

We looked around the room and I spotted it haphazardly thrown into a corner. Retrieving it, I debated commenting on the frustrations he must feel, having to rely on such an object for balance and transport. But one look at his expression as he accepted the cane from me kept me silent. I could attempt discussion with him about it later; this Phantom business came first.

Holmes washed and dressed while I waited, thumbing through one of the medical texts I always carried with me.

"I spoke with Miss Daae yesterday," Holmes said, emerging from the washroom.

"Yesterday? Holmes, you left to speak with her when I first fell ill."

"Yes. Wasn't that only yesterday?"

"No, that was four days ago."

Holmes blinked, obviously shocked. "Four days! Damn. I've lost time I can't afford to lose. Come, Watson, I'll summarize Miss Daae's account of things on the way."

So we were off to the opera house again, this time to speak with the stagehands who knew Joseph Buquet and worked on the sets for various operas. Holmes was most interested in the ones who worked on *Il Muto* and *Hannibal*. Yet no matter who he questioned or how, they all insisted they'd been at their posts, and nowhere near the set piece that had nearly squashed Carlotta, nor near the tethering ropes and chains for the chandelier. The only one who was the least bit helpful was a man named Fosse, who told us that Buquet's post had been the catwalk above the stage the night he was killed. Holmes was elated, and that was how we soon found ourselves on that same catwalk.

"Holmes, are you sure we should be out here?" I asked nervously. After all, we were a good hundred or so feet above the stage. I did not usually suffer from any sort of vertigo, but looking down gave me a distinct feeling of unease and dizziness. Holmes, on the other hand, seemed as comfortable as one with wings. He strode out to the edges, grasping for ropes to inspect, lowering himself to his good knee to check for any odd footprints on the grated floor. His cane actually became very useful, for the ropes that were just out of his reach could be gotten simply by extending that cane.

We worked our way from one end of the stage to the other, very slowly, though our lack of speed was for two very different reasons. Holmes wanted every minuscule detail recorded in his mind, and did not dare increase his momentum for fear of missing the slightest clue. I, on the other hand, simply had no desire to misstep and fall a hundred-odd feet to my death. When we reached the opposite end of the walkway, Holmes let out a soft cry of exuberance.

"Watson!" he cried, not realizing that in my mounting paranoia, I'd assumed he had lost his footing and was about to plummet to the stage below. Carefully, I sat down in the middle of the walkway and took a few slow, deep breaths. "Watson? Are you all right?"

"Holmes, if you ever let out a cry like that again when we're this far up in the air, you may just find me dead of a heart attack behind you."

He gave a hearty laugh and clapped me on the shoulder gently. "I apologize, Watson. But I'm rather excited over this discovery. Do you realize that I've found what our Phantom friend used to get here?"

I looked where he pointed to the very thin frame of a door. Unless someone was looking for it, it could not be seen. Amazingly, I pointed out the flaw in his logic. "Holmes, what if this is just a costume or prop storage area?"

"It's not. Observe," he said as he knocked on the wall in several different places. Finally, he apparently found whatever mechanism he was searching for, because the door popped open. He gestured for me to go in first and when I did, I saw a very small crawlspace with nothing inside but a chair and a black cape swirled around it.

"Evidence of our resident Phantom?" Holmes questioned, grinning at me.

I backed out of the space. "Yes, I suppose it is. But how do you know he was here when the chandelier came down?"

"Because this area is high enough that if there was another passageway in the crawlspace ceiling, it would conceivably lead to the roof. The Phantom must have been here when Carlotta's voice gave out, because as Madame Giry told us, he made his appearance known to those onstage as well as in the audience. And I'm quite sure--" Holmes stopped, then walked a few steps towards the middle of the catwalk and let out a short shout. His cry echoed through the theatre, causing several construction workers to glance up.

"Precisely. Then, if you'll look back at the wall here, Watson," Holmes said, coming closer to the doorway, "you'll notice that there are marks where something obviously made of metal was held, and as you can see, was torn out of the wall. Hmm. Whoever repaired this did a horrible job." He looked at me. "This was a holder for one of the chains for the chandelier."

I stared at the spot. Indeed, it looked as if something metal had been there previously and Holmes was right; it was a sloppily done repair.

"This can't have been the only holder for the chandelier, though," I commented.

"Of course not. But I believe this was the main one that held most of the weight. With this one gone or severely loosened, the chandelier's own weight could conquer the rest of the ropes or chains and pull itself down.

"And after what Erik heard on the roof, I'm quite sure he escaped into his crawlspace, came out here, and released the chandelier from its main hold."

"And what did he hear on the roof?" I asked.

"Miss Daae informed me that she and the Vicomte De Chagny disappeared there after Buquet's body came down. And she confided in him the secrets she had seen when the Phantom took her to wherever he lives. When she was through, the young fool tried to convince her she had only been dreaming; as if Erik's very existence was nothing more than a nightmare. She told me he made his confession of love, telling her that he could take her away from all this darkness, he could give her the sun itself. And she indulged in these fanciful whims, much to Erik's dismay, declaring her own love for Raoul."

"Oh, no . . ." I murmured.

"Yes. It seems you were right, suggesting Erik's actions have been driven by love for Miss Daae. So grief-stricken was he that in his blind anger, he descended back to this catwalk and released the chandelier. I'm sure you remember Madame Giry's telling us that maniacal laughter was heard just before it dropped."

"Indeed, but I . . . Holmes, I'm not usually right about these things! Erik is in love with Christine Daae?"

"So it would seem. But we've lingered here too long, and I believe I need another of your wonderful sedatives."

"Of course. Let us go to lunch. I'll give you something when we retire to the hotel afterwards, because I'm afraid my bag is in our room. Do you believe you can wait that long?"

"I should be able to. Sitting for a bit may prove to be all I need. After all, we've been up here for quite some time."

We made our descent back to the ground floor where Andre and Firmin were waiting for us.

"The Masquerade will take place after all!" an elated Andre announced.

"Our repairs will be finished in time and Mr.

Holmes, Dr. Watson, we'd like both of you to attend," Firmin told us.

"I look forward to it," Holmes replied without missing a beat. "And when is this festive celebration?"

"In another month, after the new chandelier is delivered and installed."

"Are you sure acquiring a new one is a good idea, gentlemen?" I asked.

A nervous, doubtful look passed over the managers' faces, but left quickly. "Not to worry," Andre said. "For this one is much smaller than the other. Besides, the Phantom wouldn't dare try that trick again."

"Really?" Holmes said, his eyebrows raised. "Well, gentlemen, I'm afraid we were just leaving. This investigation is very trying, I'm sure you understand."

"Oh, of course, please excuse us. We need to speak with our patron, anyway."

"Who is your patron, out of curiosity?" Holmes asked.

"Why, the Vicomte De Chagny, of course. We made that announcement long ago, when we first began running things here. But of course, I do apologize, you weren't present back then."

"Interesting. Good day, then." Holmes limped his way towards the door and I followed.

"Holmes, what interest is the patron to us?" I asked when we were safely within the walls of a carriage.

"What interest--? Watson, really! The Vicomte De Chagny, Raoul, Christine's childhood friend and first love--he is the patron. We will have to speak to him sooner than I thought."

"But if he doesn't believe this Phantom exists, what use can he be to us?"

"He is the third in the love triangle that is set up within those walls."

The Masquerade, as I Recall it

Unfortunately, since discovering that doorway on the catwalk, I had little success talking to anyone involved in the opera, except La Carlotta, a mammoth woman with a voice to match. Two minutes into talking with her, I could tell that she had next to no finesse in her voice. She substituted volume for style, vibrato for purity of tone, culminating in a very unpleasant experience, especially when I stupidly told her I possessed some musical knowledge. I was forced to sit through her rendition of several scales and part of an aria.

Afterward, she insisted upon regaling me with her history at the Opera Populaire, climaxing with the horrible night when 'the Phantom came to ruin her.' I know in other tales Watson has given to the public, I was reported to be a master at hiding my appearance and altering my reactions. I only hope I did that acting talent justice when I spoke with Carlotta, because that woman ground on my last nerve. It didn't surprise me in the least that the previous manager had retired for health reasons.

Carlotta made sure to inform me before I made my

escape that she would be coming to the Masquerade ball. She made mention that it would be her first public appearance since her 'humiliation' the night of *Il Muto,* and she expected to be extremely well received. She nearly trapped me in a promise of giving her the first dance, but apologetically accepted my refusal when I gave a deliberate gesture toward my leg.

It was the first time since the accident I was glad to have to rely on a cane.

I remember the Masquerade Ball very well. It was my first instance of coming face-to-face with our clever friend. I had procured costumes for both Watson and myself, though I doubt he appreciated my choice for him.

"A Harlequin clown? Holmes, why on earth should I dress up like this?" he demanded as he held up the, quite honestly, ridiculous costume.

"It lets you attend without giving away one shred of your true identity."

"Indeed," he replied. "Because after I wear this, I may never show my face to French society again!"

"Watson, I know it's a bit garish--"

"A bit!"

"--but it is necessary to remain unidentifiable, especially tonight. Erik has shown that he is capable of violence. I will not take any chances that someone I regard as a dear friend could be physically harmed."

"Holmes, does he even know we exist?"

No. Any harm would be purely accidental. Still, I will not take the chance. The Phantom will undoubtedly single out Christine and I want to be there when he does. I want to understand this spell he casts over every audience he's near. But you must fade into the background."

"How are you so sure that the Phantom will even come to tonight's spectacle?"

"It's a pattern of his. He has not always appeared where the populace can see him, but he's always there for big events. The rehearsal for *Hannibal* which was Andre and Firmin's first show as managers, the production of *Il Muto,* where they defied his wishes, and he will be here. The managers are fools who believe their office provides some security from the Phantom; they couldn't be more wrong. But that is the only reason they have been able to withstand his demands to any degree. That, and until recently, I truly believe they were more afraid of that screeching harpy they call a diva.

"Now, please, Watson, get into your costume while I change into mine."

I left the room to change and prepare for that night. I felt I'd picked a perfect costume, even more so since my cane could be integrated into it. I didn't know what was going to happen, but everything intellectually and instinctually told me that Erik would be there in the flesh instead of just behind the scenes. I was sure I would surprise him by not falling under the same pseudo-catatonia that everyone else did in his presence.

Watson and I descended the grand staircase and followed several others into the main ballroom where the Masquerade took place. The room was exquisitely decorated, with sixteen shimmering smaller chandeliers hanging in two rows from the vast ceiling. Though there were songs of merriment surrounding us and I heard many praising the arrival of the new chandelier, I also saw many glancing about furtively at the ones in this room, as if they expected one of them to fall as well.

The ball went along pleasantly until Christine and someone I could only assume was the vicomte arrived. They appeared in the middle of the festivities, Christine an absolute vision in a pink lacy dress, silver tiara, and light purple mask bedecked with jewels. Raoul accompanied her down the stairs in the outfit of a soldier, the jacket undoubtedly bearing the de Chagny coat of arms. His black mask had a very interesting pattern of stones at the outer corners of the eyes and on either side of the nose.

They danced together several times and I found myself circling the room, each rotation bringing me closer to them. They, or rather *she,* would be Erik's main target, I knew.

It was incredibly noticeable when the Phantom appeared. He was standing at the top of the grand staircase, dressed as Red Death, from the Edgar Allan Poe story. A red suit, engulfed by a large, billowing robe covered his torso, arms, and legs. On his head was a wide-brimmed hat with an impossibly large red plume. Covering his entire face was the mask of a skull. Two red eyes burned from within. Gasps and a few frightful screams, assuredly from ladies, accompanied acknowledgment of his arrival. Many backed away from him, parting as the Red Sea had for Moses. (I find I like that clever little simile, considering Erik's costume. Red Death and Red Sea.)

Christine, on the other hand, stayed frozen where she was, an interesting mix of fascination and fear on her face. Raoul backed an arm's length away, but did not let go of his love's hand.

I distinctly recall watching Erik's eyes scrutinizing every member of the audience in front of him. I purposely averted my gaze, not wanting to draw his attention by being the one face in the crowd to meet his eyes straight on. When he, I'm sure, believed he'd sufficiently intimidated everyone in the room, he began a slow descent on the stairs, mocking the managers with questions about missing their Opera Ghost.

"Have you missed me, messieurs? Did you truly believe I was gone from your midst? Am I such a spectre that you actually trusted I would disappear entirely?" He let out a mocking laugh. Then, he pulled a musical score out of his robe and tossed it so it landed at Andre's feet. "I have written you an opera. *Don Juan Triumphant,* I call it. You," he pointed at both managers, "will perform it here."

Firmin stepped forward and looked like he was going to object when Erik looked at him coldly. "I advise you to comply, Monsieur Firmin. You should not incur my wrath any further than you already have. After all, there are worse things than a shattered chandelier."

I saw both Firmin and Andre shiver at the notion. It had taken them six months to recover from the damage the chandelier had caused. They could afford no other 'accidents.'

Firmin stepped back silently, defeated. Andre picked up the score gingerly, as if it might somehow come alive.

Erik turned to Christine then and he noticed something that I had failed to see. There was a silver ring with a diamond in it on a silver chain around her neck. Instantly, I realized what that meant, as did the Phantom. He seemed to glide up to her, his long fingers going to her neck ever so gently. In one quick motion, he grabbed Raoul's ring from her neck, breaking the delicate chain, and growled in such a guttural voice that I had trouble deciphering the words, *"Your* chains are still mine. You belong to *me!"*

He was turning to go up the stairs, and I was therefore out of his line of sight when I decided to step forward. "Monsieur! Do not leave us so soon!" I called.

Erik turned and Christine stared at me as if I was

addled. The crowd stepped away, forming a ten or so foot diameter circle around me. Dimly, I was aware that Raoul had disappeared into the crowd. "Monsieur Phantom," I said, "do not leave us so quickly! You give us this warning and order, then refuse to stay for the festivities?"

"And who are you, Grim Reaper?" he asked, taking a step closer to me. "Have you come to claim my soul? You may ask anyone here, I'm sure they will tell you that is one thing I'm lacking."

I stepped closer to him and Christine backed away into the sea of faces as they gave the Phantom and me an even wider berth. "You lack more than that, dear Phantom."

"Oh? And who are you to say that to me?"

I threw off my Grim Reaper hood and stood tall before him, appearing to barely lean on the scythe-cane I had. "My name is Sherlock Holmes. I was hired to investigate the different mischievous deeds you've committed here since the production of *Hannibal.*" I extended my hand. "It is a pleasure to meet so worthy an adversary."

To this day, I wonder if the Phantom would have shaken my hand and so many events afterward could have been altered. But alas, that young fool of a vicomte had weaved through the crowd to get his sword and he came back in swinging just as the uncertainty left Erik's eyes.

Raoul is no master swordsman. He let out too much of a warning grunt when he initially attacked the Phantom. Erik was well-armed himself and before Raoul's blow fell, Erik had his own sword up and blocked. He kicked Raoul's hand and disarmed him easily, pointing the sword at his chest. Raoul backed up immediately, I hoped sensing his own foolishness. Then the Phantom pulled something else out of his robe, let it drop, and as the cloud of red smoke appeared, he vanished.

Everyone seemed frozen in their spots for a few long moments after the Phantom disappeared and the smoke dissipated. Slowly, we came back to life, began moving again. When murmuring resumed in the crowd, I grabbed the vicomte behind the elbow with my left hand and clumsily (for I was in a hurry, but my leg rarely let me hurry,) pulled him to the side, away from other people. Watson materialized from the crowd and joined me on my other side as I guided Raoul away. When I felt we were sufficiently out of hearing range, I roughly threw his arm down and whirled on him.

"You idiot! Did you think you were clever? Did you honestly expect to best the Phantom?"

Raoul sneered at me. "And what can you do with a sword?" he demanded.

"Even as I am now, I am many times the fencer you've shown yourself to be. You have no style, no finesse. You blindly attacked, and what I can or cannot do with a sword is of no consequence, as I was trying to politely talk to the man."

"He is no man! He is a monster, as Christine herself has testified. And no monster is worth talking to. *People,*" he spit out the word as if it wasn't worthy to describe Erik, "like him are useless to attempt to reason with."

"Spoken like a truly close-minded child," I replied calmly.

Raoul's face turned very red, as though he were trying to decide whether to abandon his etiquette training and begin a physical fight with me, or continue to parry with words. Though I hesitated to persist in a battle of wits, seeing as this boy was woefully unarmed.

Luckily, he didn't have to make up his mind. Christine approached us and threw herself between myself and the vicomte.

"Monsieur! Monsieur Holmes! What were you trying to do?"

Raoul looked at her in amazement. "You know this man?"

"Of course! This is the detective the managers hired. Your patronage is helping fund his investigation." She turned back to me. "Please, monsieur Holmes, what were you trying to do?"

"That is precisely what I'd like to know!" Raoul said indignantly, not seeming to care who I was.

Christine turned on him angrily. "Raoul, how could *you* be so stupid?! Why were you trying to attack Erik?"

"Why was I-- Christine, surely you understand with an opportunity like that under my nose, it would have been foolish not to take it?"

"But you're the one who looks a fool," Watson said. "Holmes was talking to him. Could have possibly gotten him to a position where he could be apprehended."

"Then you came in, trying to be a hero!" Christine yelled. She pounded her small fists on Raoul's chest.

"And how could this man be apprehended?" Raoul

demanded. "Everyone keeps talking about what a mysterious and ghostly presence he has, how he can escape any situation. If he had not been a coward, we could have duelled and seen how well he fared in an honest battle."

"As I already said, you mindless fool, I can out-fence you easily, even as I am today. You are lucky he simply disarmed you rather than choosing to duel. Considering his feelings for Miss Daae, I have no doubt that he would not have hesitated to remove you as competition for her hand, had you actually fought." I made as if to turn away from him, but turned back a second later. "You attacked remarkably fast for someone who didn't even believe Erik existed."

Raoul blinked, silenced for the first time. Before he could recover and open his mouth again, I excused Watson and myself. The Masquerade Ball was spoiled for me and I would not have the chance to search for any clues with all the other people milling around.

The day after the ball, the opera house was almost empty. Everyone was leaving it to the cleaning staff to make the Populaire spotless enough to be worth being seen in again. I used this to my advantage and investigated the spot below the grand staircase where the Phantom had dropped his smoke ball and disappeared. While I found the outline of the trapdoor he used, I could find no trigger mechanism. It irked me, but at that moment, there was nothing more that I could do.

Instead of leaving, I found myself wandering around the opera house, eventually ending up in front of the managers' office. Inside, voices were growing in volume.

"Ludicrous! Have you seen the score?"

"Utter lunacy!" Then the voice took on a hesitant quality. "Dare we refuse?"

I could not hear the muted response, but the next thing shouted was, "Not *another* chandelier!"

I opened the door. "I trust, gentlemen, you're debating the merits of performing the Phantom's opera?"

They turned and stared at me. "Were you listening at the door?"

"I was keen to investigate some of the events from the Masquerade and as I was passing by, I heard raised voices within."

"What do you suggest we do?" Andre asked.

Gazing down on his desk, I saw two cream-colored envelopes. "Look what we have here," I murmured. "Might not these be two new notes from the Phantom?"

Andre and Firmin eyed them with unease. "Undoubtedly," Andre answered. "But I'm rather reluctant to open mine."

Firmin sighed, grasping his. "We might as well get it over with."

They each tore into the envelopes with a certain amount of hesitance in their eyes. Andre's note instructed that they needed to find replacement instrumentalists for several people, a third trombone being one. Smiling slightly, I found myself wishing I could have heard this man play to see if I agreed with Erik. I pulled one of the chairs in front of their desk a few feet over to the corner and sat down.

Firmin's note suggested he find out which chorus members had good pitch and told him in no uncertain terms there were people to be sacked. He'd also managed to assign rather minor roles to the more popular names whose acting was . . . less than stellar.

Firmin picked up the score and threw it in my lap. "What do you make of this? You're supposed to be figuring out how we can get rid of this ungodly Phantom! He's now demanding we produce *this!* This piece of utter-_"

"Genius," I said, sifting through the pages. Yes, there were parts that were very harsh, meant to, I'm sure, cause the listeners almost physical pain, but in others, there was such gentle beauty and kindness. For several minutes I pored over the score, sight reading and, undoubtedly inadequately, humming some parts of it to myself. When I eventually looked up at the two men staring at me in confusion, I flipped back to the first page. "Gentlemen, whatever else this Phantom has done to you, he will not cause you bankruptcy when you perform this opera. If any one of your audience has a single drop of true culture in their veins, they will appreciate this piece."

I settled myself down to get a feel for the storyline when La Carlotta and Piangi burst in, Carlotta loudly voicing her outrage at the music and the size of her part. I looked up, startled, recalling the words of the note. Giving miniscule parts to big names who couldn't act. Once again, a small smile played itself across my face. The Phantom enjoyed causing mayhem among the managers and Carlotta; I was beginning to see why.

Just when Carlotta and Piangi appeared to reach their crescendo of complaints and could have (theoretically) calmed down, Christine and Raoul walked in. There was an instant uproar. Carlotta berated Christine's acquisition of the lead role and accused her of being the one behind things. Christine truly got angry then, but I noticed her face and eyes didn't match her heated words. She seemed distracted. Haunted might be a better word, considering her appearance. She was thinner than the first time I met her and her skin had none of the glow of the previous night. Dark circles were under her unfocused eyes. It seemed to me she kept glancing over her shoulder. Finally she told Andre and Firmin she wanted no part of this plot and seemed to break down under their questions until Raoul took her in his arms and comforted her.

I was the only one who heard the gentle knock on the door. Stiffly, as my leg was starting to act up again, I stood and let Madame Giry into the room. Her gaze passed over each of us as she haltingly pulled a piece of paper from an apron attached to her skirt.

"Messieurs, another note."

They all groaned, but I held out my hand. I read it

aloud, barely able to hold back something of a sarcastic laugh at parts. The Phantom singled out, save Madame Giry and Raoul, everyone in the room. He let them know that Carlotta was not to use her usual trick of strutting around the stage and calling it acting. Piangi was to lose weight before he could successfully take on his role of Don Juan. The managers had to learn that their place was in the office with the books and the money rather than in the arts. Christine, he requested to his company so he could continue to teach her, if her pride would let her return to him.

" . . . *And to the detective you've hired, I look forward to another meeting. Had our last not been interrupted, perhaps we could have come to an understanding.*" I stared meaningfully at Raoul. "*Your obedient friend, and Angel.*"

Raoul stared coldly back at me. "Understanding. This monster is not capable of such a thing!" He faced the managers. "Gentlemen, we've all been blind. The answer is right in front of us. This is our chance to outwit him!"

Andre and Firmin gave quick glances at me, but the allure of a solution was too strong, I suppose, for they leaned toward Raoul. "We're listening."

"Yes, do go on."

"We'll play his game. Perform this . . . opera . . . of his. But remember, we hold the ace!" He pointed at Christine. "If you sing, the Phantom will come."

"We'll lock the doors!" Andre cried.

"We'll get police!" Firmin added.

They met one another's eyes. "They'll be armed!"

"And his reign here will end!" Raoul finished.

In an interesting burst of dual thinking, Madame Giry and I simultaneously shouted, "Madness!" Muted, she, along with everyone else in the room, stared at me as I continued. "That is utter madness. You cannot hope to outwit one such as he with multiple men and guns. That can only end in innocent people being injured -- or killed! Do you truly want that on your conscience? Are you so obsessed with catching this Phantom that you would sacrifice innocent lives?"

"Innocent lives! The policemen of this city know how to handle themselves and their weapons. They would not fire unless ordered to," Raoul argued, "and certainly not at civilians or each other."

"You assume their minds will be perfectly clear," I said. "A common mistake in a situation like this. While under normal circumstances, you may very well be right, Vicomte, these are far from normal circumstances. How can you be sure that every one of those men will not be subject to actions dictated by fear, by panic?"

Andre shook his head. "Monsieur Holmes, I'm grateful that you have come to try and help our situation, but you've done nothing, taken no action against this man. Now, Raoul has a plan to capture him and everyone here thinks it will work, save you."

"Save me?" I said. I glanced at Madame Giry as well as Christine. "I don't believe I was the only one who said this was madness. Why don't we ask the others present if they think it will work before you make such an assumption, shall we?"

Madame Giry stepped forward. "It is madness, gentlemen, for all the reasons Monsieur Holmes stated and more. The Phantom will not be caught by simple trickery like this. He is not one who is caught by brute force. If he is to be stopped, I believe Monsieur Holmes is the best, and only, person to do it."

Her statements caused another uproar and the managers, Raoul, Carlotta, Piangi, and Madame Giry began arguing amongst themselves. I shook my head, finding it hard to believe that so many mindless fools could be in one place. I was tempted to leave, since I doubted any of them would notice my absence, when I caught the expression on Miss Daae's face. Her eyes were no longer unfocused; rather, they looked close to insanity. Finally, she let out a screech and whirled to face all of them.

"If you don't stop, I'll go mad!"

All went still. Everyone's eyes were on her as we watched her tremble. Being the quickest thinker present, I limped over and grabbed the second chair in front of the managers' desk and positioned it so Christine could fall into it comfortably. Not a moment too soon, either, for her legs gave out and she collapsed onto the cushion. When she did, Raoul knelt by her side, looking up into her face. "Christine . . ."

"Raoul," she whispered, "how can you even suggest this? I'm frightened. I don't know what he'll do. If he takes me, I'll never see you again, he'll never let me go." She gave a gentle sniff and Raoul pulled a handkerchief from his pocket to hand to her. She accepted it gratefully and pressed it to the side of her mouth and nose. "I used to dream. I used to dream my Angel of

Music would come. But I didn't want this. This is a nightmare with no end. He's . . . he's always there, singing . . . in my head . . ."

"She's mad . . ." Carlotta murmured, as if the full influence of the Phantom was just occurring to her.

Andre and Firmin gazed at her with open contempt. I'm sure they didn't want Christine to be set off into a streak of violence and if anyone here could manage exactly that, it would be Carlotta. But Christine remained sitting, and soon began talking, once again as if she was in a daze.

"Things are so twisted . . . his desires, his wants. He's given me everything I ever hoped for, but now you expect me to betray him?"

"Christine--" Raoul tried to say.

"No! You want me to be his prey and you're not giving me any choice. He's already killed a man without a second thought and you want me to agree to be in his clutches voluntarily? When all you wanted before was to get me as far away as you could? Up on the roof, you said you could order your finest horses to the gate and we'd ride off into the night. But now . . . What kind of game are you trying to play, Raoul? Would you truly go to any lengths against the Phantom, even so far as making me the bait?"

"Christine," Raoul began again, "it's not that I want to put you in danger. I want this man apprehended and having you provide a distraction while the police get him is our only chance."

I snorted lightly. While I'm sure that Raoul heard, he ignored me. Christine, however, looked at me. "Monsieur Holmes, what do you think can be done? What do you think Erik intends to do?"

I sighed. "To be honest, right now I haven't the foggiest what he could have planned. Obviously it would take place during the opera he wants you to perform. As for what can be done, well, anything I come up with would be immediately rejected in favour of the idea the vicomte has already suggested." I moved towards the door. "Because of that, I believe my services are no longer required. I'll go now. You will receive my bill tomorrow for the services I've already rendered."

"If you feel that's best, Monsieur Holmes," Firmin said. "You will be missed."

I gave a somewhat cruel smile as I muttered, "I somehow doubt that." Aloud, I told them, "I shall stay in

Paris long enough to see this opera performed. I hope, for your sakes, that the vicomte's plan is successful."

I left the office, letting their fresh outburst fall on deaf ears. When I was barely twenty feet down the hall, Madame Giry caught my arm. "You surely are not leaving this to Raoul's hopeless idea? He can be a very kind person, but this is far beyond him."

"Of that, I'm well aware, my dear woman. That is why I must find the Phantom before this plot has a chance to misfire. Now, if you'll excuse me, I must leave."

She had a puzzled expression on her face as I turned away again, but before I could take a step, the office door opened and Madame Giry and I heard a strangled cry from the doorway. Christine was rushing towards us and I managed to catch her arm with my left hand.

"Miss Daae! Please, what has come over you?"

She couldn't answer, she was sobbing so hard. But then I heard my answer. From within the office, I heard the vicomte shout, "So it *is* to be war between us. But this time, 'clever' friend, the disaster will be *yours.*"

"That fool," I muttered.

Raoul

I don't believe in ghosts.

However, my childhood friend and sweetheart has been taken in by one. Or by someone pretending to be one. Her Angel of Music. Bah! There was only one Angel of Music, and it's not this phony she claims sings to her through her full-length dressing room mirror. It was a figment in the imagination of Christine's father, a world-renowned violinist. All the stories he wove while masterfully playing the violin involved this Angel, this muse who would descend on especially gifted singers or dancers.

But Christine has taken this foolishness too far. She actually has the audacity to tell others this 'Angel of Music' is her teacher. My efforts to capture her attentions and favour were rebuffed many times because of *his* insistence regarding her vigilance.

But no more! An idea has taken shape in my mind. An idea to capture this Phantom fiend . . . Christine is not fond of it, but she will obey. She refuses to admit it, she's even denied it, but she wants this monster out of her life as much as I do.

I can only hope that fool detective the managers hired won't stand in my way. He claims to have taken himself off the case, but I know better. He wishes to thwart me, though what gain it will get him, I cannot imagine. He surely does not wish to take Christine for himself and he has nothing to gain by imagining he can take this Phantom on by himself. Someone who has the power to delude almost everyone in this opera house into thinking he has some great measure of power against someone who cannot walk in a straight line without the assistance of a cane? Someone who called me a child on more than one occasion? I say without hesitation that Sherlock Holmes is a fool of the highest calibre, thinking that he, a single man, is more powerful than an entire police force.

*   *   *

I hardly consider this worth its own section, but one of the papers I found when searching was something Raoul wrote. Christine must have left it with me at some point. I can think of no other reason I would have it. I suppose he took his thoughts to paper after leaving the office. Looking over it, I must admit, I'm amused by his perception of me. His musings of Christine Daae, though, are quite insulting for a man who claimed to be so smitten.

From the Journal of John H. Watson, M.D.

I dearly wish I'd been present to witness the scene in the managers' office. Unfortunately, Holmes requested I spend the day sight-seeing. I believe his exact words were, "This case has more complexities than you could imagine. One of us should have the ability to say we explored this great city and as I lost four days already, I cannot take any more time off. Take the day; I'm sure nothing eventful will happen."

That will be the last time I listen to him about a day not being eventful.

Holmes did keep his word to the managers and considered himself officially off the case. Privately, however, nothing could keep him from his investigation. I found him one night sitting at the desk in the hotel room, a miniature version of his extensive chemistry set laid out before him.

"Might I inquire what you're examining?" I asked, approaching him carefully. I was fairly knowledgeable about chemicals myself, but I could never be sure if Holmes was dabbling with poisons, antidotes, or just things to hold his interest and fend off his use of cocaine. Because of that, I always refrained from curiously touching anything of his in this field.

"Of course you may," he said, holding what looked to be threads pinched by a pair of tweezers in one hand and carefully dabbing a solution on to them from a tissue in his other.

I gave him an exasperated look. "What are you examining, Holmes?"

He glanced at me and grinned. "I'm glad you asked. I found this the second day I was at the opera house, when I spoke with Miss Daae while you were ill. I got a chance before seeing her to explore Box five, and this was wedged in the seat."

"Threads were lodged in the seat?"

"Not just threads. It was a slightly bigger piece of cloth. Roughly three inches by six inches, so I would guess. It ripped on an angle."

"But what is it? Aside from a piece of cloth that has held your interest for a remarkably long time now."

"Watson, come now! You surely should be able to piece this together. I found it in Box five. The only one we know of to ever sit in Box five is . . . ?"

"The Phantom!" I exclaimed, feeling utterly foolish. "Of course, it belongs to Erik, perhaps a ripped pant leg or coattail."

"Neither. This is from a cloak. And one not worn until recently, either. I can estimate it to have been packed away until the past few months. It must be a very warm garment."

"Why do you say that?"

"Well, the weather is, and has been, cold since we've arrived here. I can deduce the cloth wasn't there for very long because even though no one sits in the box during operas, it needs to be cleaned."

"Are you quite sure a cleaning person will go in? They could be just as superstitious as the chorus girls."

"Perhaps, but even if that was the case, someone like Madame Giry would certainly go up there to make sure things were suitable. And she would notice the cloth, since she always checks the seat because that's where Erik has always left her rewards."

"Brilliant," I marvelled.

"And that's not all. I've discovered where our elusive Phantom resides. I can't believe I didn't see it before."

"And where is that?" I asked.

He lowered his hands and stared at me, the flame from underneath a Bunsen burner casting eerie shadows across his face. "Beneath the opera house."

"What?" I asked after a long bout of silence. "Holmes, really. How could anyone survive down there? It's impossible. He'd need proper shelter, food, water, a heating system--"

"And who's to say he didn't gather these things when the opera house was originally built?" Holmes challenged. "I've looked at Garnier's plans, Watson. They are so layered, if you looked at the opera house from above, it would resemble a maze, weaving in and out inside itself. I've attempted to look up the names of the contractors on the records sheets. Do you know the ones that are actually named have not been commissioned to build anything since? It appears they were paid well enough to go into retirement no matter what their age, and after they were given the money, were encouraged to leave Paris."

"What purpose could that serve?"

"That way no one could find them to question them about the lower levels of the opera house." He pulled several sheets of paper from under the desk and handed them to me. "Unroll these on the bed. I found the full square footage of the entire building, lower levels and all. Now, take a look at the map of the opera house that the managers gave me."

I settled them out next to one another on the bed and studied both very carefully for several minutes. I could barely make sense of the original plans; Holmes was right, it was a maze within a maze within a maze. But I committed the square footage to memory, then turned my gaze to the other sheet. The map was much simpler. Crude, even. And the square footage was nowhere near what the first one was.

"The lower regions weren't included," I concluded.

"Exactly. The Phantom wanted it that way. The first plan with the correct amount of space was given to me by the company Garnier talked to in order to get one of the first loans. They needed the full plan to get an idea of how much money Garnier needed. Erik must have planted the other map in the office because he didn't want the managers to have any knowledge of the secret passageways galore in the depths of the building. It would take me ages to sort out where each one is."

"Then why do you look so happy?" I asked.

"Because it may take ages to find all of them, but all I really need is one. I believe most lead, eventually, to the same place. The Phantom's lair. And Miss Daae's dressing room mirror is the entryway I shall take when I go to confirm my theory."

"Holmes . . . I'm sorry to go off subject, but I asked how he would get food and water as well as shelter. How is he getting the provisions in order to remain healthy living down there?"

"Don't you remember Madame Giry mentioning the chorus girls saying things would disappear? How often do you suppose the things that would disappear were food items? Not to mention that he receives twenty thousand francs a month. I'm sure some of that goes to a grocery boy."

I nodded. "Of course. I should have known. So, how did you arrive at the conclusion that the mirror was one of his passageways?"

"It's reasonable. She is the one who was taught by him and it had to be in a fairly discreet place, yet close to the opera. Why not inside the opera itself? And Madame Giry's words of a man's voice coming from within

Christine's dressing room? Not only should I have realized that he had secret passageways, I should have realized his home was beneath the opera house then!" He shook his head and put his chin in his hand. "Now, one problem remains."

"What's that?" I asked.

"I will not risk trying to find another passageway and hoping it leads me to him. I do not have the time. I must get back in the opera house and enter Miss Daae's dressing room. Only then will I be successful in descending to Erik's lair."

"Can you not just enter the opera house to explore?"

"No. Undoubtedly I would be stopped. Remember, I took myself off the investigation. The vicomte, especially, will not let me come near those doors again, unless I am seeing an opera. And if I were to gain entry because I was there for a performance, it's likely I'd be watched for any suspicious behaviour, including trying to sneak off to a dressing room."

Holmes tapped his cane on the floor a few times, then threw it on the second bed, an expression of disgust crossing his features. Then he crossed his arms and sat back.

"Holmes, you said I could speak frankly in front of you," I began.

"Of course. You know I want absolute honesty in my cases. Why would I expect any less from you, someone I call a dear friend?"

"Because you may not appreciate what I want to say," I countered.

"That's always a consideration, I must admit. But it's hardly a reason not to say something. Appreciation may not be immediate, but it can always come after a time."

"I suppose that's true. And this is something I've considered saying more than once since our arrival in Paris." I sighed. "Holmes, as always, your deductions and attention to detail are incredible. They never cease to amaze me. You've shown your normal foresight and skills, yet it seems you're lacking in confidence. You're right; you should have realized where the Phantom lived from Madame Giry's words. Or at least realized it was a logical place to theorize him living, considering you did not have all the facts yet. But only today are you looking on them in hindsight with the knowledge of the clue they held. Holmes, you're not at your best mentally, and I fear it has to do with not being your best physically."

As the expression on his face changed again, I found I was holding my breath. It was rare that I was so straightforward in my criticisms. Finally, he heaved a great sigh and said, "I've been considering that same problem. It's the main reason why I announced my retirement. But of course, mysteries and investigation do run through my veins and this case was far too intriguing to pass by."

"Of course. It has all the classic elements. Murder, a 'ghost,' romantic intrigue. But why does your physical state impair, or I'm guessing enhance, your mental state?"

"It doesn't. At least, not in the way I'm sure you're thinking. Watson, since getting that blasted cane, I've been defined by it. You heard the managers about not knowing they 'hired a cripple.' When Miss Daae first saw me, she identified me because I was described as using a cane."

"But that doesn't diminish your status as a detective. Or your reputation for solving these seemingly impossible crimes and situations."

"In a way, it does. If I continue solving mysteries and such now, people will remember my past reputation and wonder, 'can he still do it?' I'll not be remembered for my skills, but rather because I solved something in spite of my situation. It's not something I relish enduring."

"Not that, surely. But I'd think you would enjoy solving the case and then telling them 'I told you so,' in some non-descript way."

Holmes actually smiled. "Yes, I admit, that would be entertaining."

"You never worried about how to get into a place before. You always had an idea for some creative disguise. Fake noses, blackened teeth, wigs, false moustaches, beards, sideburns, and clothes that fit whatever part you chose to play. Could you not perform the same feat now?"

"Unfortunately, no. Once again, this cane defines me. Or more accurately, my gait. It complicates things because it minimizes the number of disguises I could reasonably use. The very way I walk now is too easily recognizable. I cannot sneak my way in."

"Let me be your eyes, then," I suggested in a rare

flash of brilliance. "I have no such ban on my entry, nor a limit to disguises I can pull off. I'll scout around and let you know when the opera is at its emptiest each day. Then we can plan our route down the mirror's passageway."

"You would do this?"

"Of course. I may not even need a costume. The managers only saw me the initial day of our arrival, when they told us the ball was still on, and then in costume at the Masquerade. I'm sure they barely glanced at me on any of the three occasions. They will have no reason to connect my presence with you."

"Indeed, they would not. Twice seeing you in regular clothing would not be enough for those two to distinguish you from the masses. Though I may dress you up with a fake moustache or perhaps a pair of spectacles. One can never be too careful. However, I'm sure you will pose no threat to them. All right, then. I'll gladly have you be my eyes and ears in the opera. You are familiar enough with my methods. Take note of the tiniest details, because they may be of utmost importance. Pay special attention to the shadows, and if you feel yourself being followed, leave. I never wanted our presence to disturb the Phantom. While it remains to be seen if Erik is truly insane, I have no doubt he's a temperamental and volatile sort."

"Never wanted to disturb--? But Holmes, what of your calling his attention at the Masquerade?"

"That was a calculated chance at an introduction. I wanted him to know of my existence. I wanted him to know I was not a person to fear. I wanted to see if we could come to an understanding, though the vicomte made sure to end that possibility before it had the chance to flourish or fail. I do not, however, want the Phantom to know quite yet exactly how thoroughly I'm investigating him and I do not want him disturbed by us. The managers do a fine job of that on their own."

"I shall be as discreet as I possibly can," I promised.

"Thank you, Watson. You are a true friend," Holmes said, looking immensely grateful.

At The Graveyard

Watson was true to his word and went to the opera house each day. The first day, he discovered beyond a glimmer of a doubt that the managers did not recognize him, so he pretended to be one of the workers who would come each day to make sure the new chandelier was still properly held in place. I must admit, it amused me to hear they were taking no chances with this one.

Also, Watson would report to me if he happened to see the vicomte or Miss Daae. Since either of them most definitely would recognize him, I insisted he present himself in something to alter his appearance. That usually meant him spending an extra twenty-odd minutes in the washroom, not only donning fake spectacles, but usually attaching fake eyebrows, sideburns, a moustache, and beard to his face. Quite often during his skulking periods, he'd witness them arguing over Raoul's plan, Christine still insisting the Phantom would take her and Raoul was willingly handing her over to the very person he wanted to save her from.

One day, about a week after Watson had begun his

spying, he burst into the hotel room, gasping for breath. "Holmes-- carriage-- go-- Erik--"

That was all I needed to hear.

The carriage approached a dark graveyard some twenty minutes later. Watson had explained to me what happened in great detail whilst peeling off the different hair pieces attached to his face. He was watching a rehearsal of *Don Juan Triumphant* in which Piangi appeared incapable of correctly singing one of his lines. Carlotta berated the Phantom's opera, saying Piangi's way of singing was better; at least he made it sound like music.

Soon, everyone onstage was in some kind of argument with another person; then something strange happened. The piano that the instructor had abandoned in order to argue with a dancer began playing of its own accord. Everyone began correctly singing their lines, as if held in a trance. Except for Miss Daae. She wandered away, murmuring something about someone singing to her in her dreams. Watson followed her outside, concerned for her well-being, when he happened to glance over at the man tending the horse at the front of the carriage.

"He had a mask on, Holmes," he told me. "It was

a white mask that appeared to cover half his face. I can think of no one else who has the need to wear a mask, so I ran here and called a carriage for the both of us, thinking you would want to investigate."

"You were right to do so," I told him.

The Phantom wouldn't be the driver. He'd want to be positioned in the graveyard before Christine arrived. But I knew in my very soul that he'd told the true driver where to take her.

Watson and I got out of our carriage at the edge of the only logical graveyard someone from the opera house would head to, and I told the driver to head on his way. Carefully, we waded through waist-deep weeds, marshy puddles, and around cement gravestones (none of which were easy to navigate with a cane) until we stood behind a grand mausoleum. Watson was still moving forward when I heard the voice. I quickly held my cane out in front of him to stop him from going any further.

"Yes, come to me, my dear. Come to your Angel . . ." a voice was murmuring.

"The Phantom," Watson breathed, barely louder than a sigh. I nodded and glanced at my cane in contempt. I desperately wanted to get closer, but damn this infernal cane, I didn't dare because I couldn't do so silently!

There were distant footsteps that seemed to approach the mausoleum and then Christine's voice carried over the wind. She was singing, though I couldn't make out any words. The melody was beautiful, haunting. When she was through, violin music began to waft through the air. The wind died down to nothingness; everything was still. I have never heard the violin, or any instrument, played with such majesty, such absolute control and mastery. Of course I'd heard technically perfect playing. That is, matching a finely tuned instrument with a player who could hit all the right notes for the correct lengths of time. But this, this music was soulfully perfect. It grasped my heart and twisted, leaving me yearning for more. I truly believed I had never heard real music until that moment. Something in me knew I would consider all future attempts as merely noise, compared with this.

Even more surprising, the violinist soon began to sing back to Christine.

"Wandering child, so lost, so helpless . . ."

He had a rich baritone voice with a superb high range. I now knew what Christine meant about having the voice of an angel. How long must this man have trained to have attained such a miraculous grasp on his vocal cords?

"I denied you . . ." Christine murmured in an almost sleep-like state. Her voice harmonized with the Phantom's as they both sang, "Turning from true beauty!"

"Raoul," Watson barely whispered, pointing to the left. I looked and indeed, Raoul was fast approaching. Luckily, he had no weaponry on him. From our vantage point, we watched as the vicomte fearlessly, or stupidly, depending on how one viewed Raoul, kept walking towards the mausoleum. When he got nowhere trying to break the spell over Christine, he mocked the Phantom. Yet one thing he said, I could not deny: *"You can't win her love by making her your prisoner."*

Finally, the Phantom began shooting small fireballs at Raoul's feet, deriding the vicomte, asking how far he'd dare go, when Christine seemed to break from the Phantom's spell. She fell into Raoul's arms and then looked back at the Phantom, terror and fascination spelled out in her eyes. Christine got to her feet, took Raoul's hand, and pulled him away. When the Phantom realized he was losing her, he shouted, "Don't go!"

But as they disappeared into the night, he cried after them, *"So be it! Now let it be war upon you both!"*

His great shout echoed into the night as Christine and Raoul were engulfed by darkness. I could nearly feel the emotional pain I knew the Phantom to be in. Memories engulfed me, bringing me back to the period of my life when my heart was shattered. I raised my hand, wanting somehow to comfort him. But with my hand just above shoulder level, my brain decided to wake back up, letting logic overcome emotion. I dropped my arm back to my side. What was I thinking? Was it Erik's musical genius? Had it cast a spell on even me? Or perhaps the macabre setting, allowing me to fall back into fancy, something I never allowed myself to do.

Or was it his palpable pain that let me relate so poignantly?

I had no time to dwell on those speculations, for Erik turned and jumped off the mausoleum, landing, crouched, in the tall grass in front of us. As he stretched to his full height, I noticed again, as I had at the Masquerade, that he stood a good four inches taller than I did.

"You," he rasped as I stared directly into his eyes.

"You spoke to me at the Masquerade. Why have you followed me to the cemetery?"

"The better question," I said slowly, weighing my words carefully, "is why you lured Christine here."

"The facts are in front of you, Detective," he said derisively. He straightened his right arm and planted the cane the fireballs had come from in the marshy ground. I must admit, I had to admire how quickly he composed himself. "By all means, figure out my motives. Join the vicomte in his foolish attempt to capture me. But I assure you--"

"Yes, yes, I'm quite certain of his imminent failure. You need not convince me of that, nor insult me by assuming I want anything to do with his childish plan," I interrupted, mirroring his movements by extending my left arm and planting my own cane in the ground.

"You do not wish to capture me?" Erik asked.

"If I did, I would have done so by now."

"Are you quite sure of that, Detective? Could you chase me through the underground labyrinth I constructed?"

Erik was trying to defeat me by emotional means. Unrecognized, he could conceivably weave someone's thoughts in and out however he pleased. I was not such an easy foe to sidetrack, though. And I hoped he didn't know the extent to which I relied on this cane. I wouldn't give him any more information than was needed concerning that.

"I would have no need to chase you. I would arrive first at your predetermined destination."

"Arrogance! And quite possibly the intelligence to back up your claims. A welcome change from the snivelling vicomte's whiny protests. You would arrive first, you say? Would you care to make a wager on that?"

"No, thank you. I'm receiving quite enough of the opera house's money. I don't need more of it from you." Two could play at emotionally driven mind games.

Erik's eyes widened, then narrowed. "Perhaps I have underestimated you. All right. I offer you an equitable chance, then. Shall we settle this fairly, say with a fencing match?"

He clearly had no idea how completely this bothersome cane had become a part of my person. Carefully, keeping the hesitation and yes, even fear out of my voice and expression, I slowly nodded and answered, "Name your time and place."

"Tonight. Midnight. The stage of the Opera Populaire. I shall gain you entry. Let us see how our skills compare."

"Very well. But what are the rules of engagement? And what of the victor and the loser?" I asked.

"Rules of engagement are simply those we learned when training for swordplay. The victor and the loser? Only one shall walk away with his life. A fight to the death, Monsieur Holmes."

"You expect that I could kill you?"

He chuckled cruelly. "Again your arrogance shows."

"Not at all," I said. "I have no doubt you could kill me. You have proven to have no qualms about ending the life of a fellow man. However, I have no such lack of inhibition. Do you truly expect that I could kill you?"

The Phantom considered for a long moment. "Perhaps not. True, you do not seem the sort willing to drive a sword through a man's heart. I admit, the finesse for killing is more my forte. If you best me in sword fighting, you will not be expected to have my blood on your hands. I assure you I will abandon my plans for Christine Daae and leave the opera house."

"For how long?"

"Forever."

"It is your home."

"It is my prison. My own gate to Hell. It would be foolish for you to assume I could not find a portal in another location."

"Of course. Hence why I never make assumptions. But on account that I win, I have no interest in taking you from the place you've dwelled for the past fifteen odd years. Not to mention that I have no wish to 'kill' whatever emotions you have left to feel."

The Phantom's eyes took on a gleam of curiosity. "You discerned that. Regardless, you must do one or the other at midnight tonight. Otherwise, Christine Daae is mine, the vicomte and his foolish plans be damned!"

Before I could react, the Phantom had disappeared into the dark with a swish of his cloak and a brilliant flash of light from the cane.

"Damn!" I shouted, tempted to throw my cane at the spot Erik had occupied only seconds before. But of course, I was near helpless without it on this terrain.

"Well. It seems I won't have to worry about finding a way to the mirror now." I turned to look at

Watson and saw the stricken expression across his features. With that, the desperation of my situation truly hit me. "Watson . . ."

"Yes, Holmes?" he murmured in a fear-filled whisper.

"I haven't fenced since before the infernal accident. Despite what I asserted to the vicomte, I'm unsure of my ability to even *hold* a sword competently anymore. What in Hell am I supposed to do?"

"Could it have been a bluff? He can't truly mean to kill you," Watson tried to suggest.

I smiled cruelly and turned away. Watson's optimism did me no good now. "He means it. The Phantom would not stage a bluff. I have an immense amount of respect for him and I believe he respects me in turn, which is why he has offered me this chance to best him fairly. Yet he won't hold back. He wants his plan to proceed and he is willing to eliminate any and all hitches." I closed my eyes. "And I, my friend, am a hitch."

From the Journal of John H. Watson, M.D.

After the scene at the graveyard, Holmes and I walked slowly back to our hotel. I worried over him travelling such a distance; after all, if he did intend to fence with the Phantom, he needed as much strength and mobility as possible, and extended use of his leg now tired him out and made moving quite painful. I dared not say anything, though. He had too much on his mind to be bothered by my worries, even ones meant for his well-being.

Back at the hotel, he stretched out on one of the beds, grimacing as he brought his right leg up on several pillows he'd carefully positioned. He sat back and let his head loll against the headboard. Several times I wanted to ask him what his plan was, but something told me he was still formulating it, so I remained silent.

At precisely eleven, Holmes eased himself into a standing position. "Watson, I do not ask that you accompany me."

"I would not think of failing to be at your side now."

"Think over your choice carefully. After all, it may well be that I go to my death tonight."

"Holmes, do you truly believe that?" I asked incredulously.

He grasped the head of his cane and went to the door. "Unfortunately, I do. I will try to talk to him first, see if we can parry words and come to an understanding, instead of blades and being brought to death. However, I'm fairly certain I will fail. I understand him almost to perfection at this point. His motives, his methods, the ironies that constantly surround him in the opera house. But the idea of articulating those ideas into an outlook he would listen to . . . That's entirely a different matter."

Again the thought plagued me that he would not have such a black outlook on his fate if he had full use of his body. But then, while I knew Holmes would go to any length to protect himself from harm, he would not hurt or kill someone else unless he had no other choice. And maimed leg or not, he didn't feel this was a situation of 'kill or be killed,' despite the fact that the Phantom presented it that way.

*　　　　　*　　　　　*

Holmes did not even glance at the main door of the opera house when we approached the building at the stroke of midnight. I couldn't fathom what he was looking for, but I noticed an irritating light continually blinking on and off that seemed to captivate him. After a solid five minutes of him staring at the spot from which the light was coming, he finally turned to me and said, "There's a back way. A passageway the Phantom built that will lead us in and to the stage. It's on the other side of the building."

Shocked, I looked at Holmes, then to the opera house. "How the devil did you know that?" I asked.

He pointed his thumb to the place the light had flashed from. "Morse code, from Erik."

I blinked in amazement and began to understand Holmes's despair in the face of such a being. Yet from what I discerned of both men, they were extraordinarily alike! Both jack-of-all-trades, both something of an outcast from their worlds yet remarkably well-known within them, and since Holmes's accident, they were now both maimed in some life-altering way.

As Holmes and I made our way to the other side of the opera house, I found myself wishing that he and the

Phantom could come to an understanding before blades were drawn.

Our Swordfight

I dearly wish that I had Watson's recollection of this event. The idea of having a third person perspective on our duel quite honestly thrilled me. But alas, this was also one of the most dramatic events of our stay in Paris and Watson was probably relying on his memory while he wrote out what he considered to be some of the more mundane parts of the tale. Then I insisted I didn't want him to publish these events and in an effort to not let anything slip to the public, he ceased his writings immediately. I must admit, I'm exceptionally glad he only ceased his writings and didn't destroy them.

I don't remember entering the opera house. I only vaguely recall the Morse code message Erik gave me as Watson and I waited outside. The first clear thing I do recall is descending the long aisle from the back of the auditorium to the foot of the stage. There was a lone black chair placed in the middle, it's back to us, and a single spotlight shining on it. As I watched, the Phantom's hand appeared on the left armrest and he stood, turning to face us, his cape swirling in a graceful arc about his legs.

"Monsieur Holmes. A pleasure to see you," he said, a slight snarl in his tone despite the polite words.

"Did you expect me to bow out? Perhaps you assumed I was a coward," I said.

"Perhaps. But wasn't it you who let me know, in no uncertain terms, that one should never assume anything?"

I gave a sardonic grin, and a slight bow to the Phantom. "Touché. You do not mind that we shall have an audience for the swordfight?" I gestured to Watson, who readily stepped up next to me. "This is my good friend, doctor John Watson. Watson, of course by now you're familiar with Erik-- I'm sorry, I do not know your last name."

Erik looked genuinely surprised that anyone should care. "I have no surname. I left my mother years ago and have no wish to remember her. So I am only Erik."

I moved away from Watson and stepped closer to the stairs that would get me on the stage. "Only? You are far from 'only' anything! I heard you play in the cemetery. You had complete mastery of that violin. I would even go so far as to say it was a living creature; that your minds had become one. You gave a brilliant performance. It is a shame to waste such talent on hypnotizing young girls."

The Phantom's eyes flashed. "So that is your game, Sherlock Holmes? Flatter my abilities, charm me with your talk of my talents, and then mock the way I choose to use them?"

Blast, he was quick! I would have to be more careful. I extended my hand to grasp the railing at the foot of the stairs and said sincerely, "Mocking? I am by no means mocking you. I'm merely commenting that a musical genius such as yourself shouldn't lower himself to calling out to chorus girls in a graveyard."

"You know nothing of Christine's and my past," he hissed.

"Perhaps not. But I know you. I feel I have a very acute understanding of your character, Erik."

"Do you? And how have you grasped such an extensive knowledge?"

"I've extracted bits and pieces from here and there. Numerous sources. Garnier's notes about the construction, Madame Giry's stories about the gypsy carnival, the tales floating around here about the 'opera ghost,' the story of the fallen chandelier and the maniacal laughter heard just before its descent, even the sense of devotion yet fear from Miss Daae when she's spoken of her Angel of Music. Though I must admit, Madame Giry's stories are the ones I find most relevant now."

"Really. And why is that?"

I was now on the stage and working my way toward Erik, taking slow, calculated steps. I knew what I wanted to say just as I approached him. "Before I explain, please enlighten me on something."

"That would be?"

"Why did you kill Joseph Buquet?"

The Phantom laughed. "That repugnant excuse for a man enjoyed toying with the chorus girls. Not just the usual teasing manner that most stagehands employ; this man would rape them with his eyes."

I stopped, shocked. Others had spoken of being disgusted with the man before, but no one had said such candid, and so despicable, things about him.

Erik continued. "More than once, I'm sure, he carried it beyond what his eyes and imagination could do. During rehearsals for *Il Muto,* I heard him speak of Christine in a vulgar way, saying, in far less refined terms, how much he'd like to get his hands on her. I decided to keep an eye on him.

"During the performance, I was up in the catwalks, as was he. He was drinking, and after the announcement that Christine was to take the place as the countess, Buquet said to another man how he wanted to sneak down and watch Christine change. To see her naked body and perhaps run his fingers over it."

My eyes widened. In Erik's position, I would find it hard to have the self-control needed to not knock the man unconscious.

"After I heard that, I saw red at the edges of my vision and I knew the only way to appease my sight was to see Buquet's blood. So I followed him. I caught him easily and when I did I slashed his throat, wrapped a rope around his neck, and tossed him down."

"God knows Christine's fate if you hadn't acted," I murmured, more to myself than to him.

He heard me, however. "Yes. He was a repulsive excuse for a man, but I would not have killed him had he not wanted to defile my Christine."

"I do not agree with murder, and you have undeniably committed that act, but I agree with your sentiments," I said as I began walking again. "I said I would enlighten you on why I found Madame Giry's stories the most interesting. And your tale of Joseph Buquet only corroborates my thoughts."

"Which are?"

"You escaped from the gypsy carnival by killing the cruel man who held you prisoner. You killed Buquet because he was a genuine threat to Christine. But how many times have the managers disobeyed you? Raoul holds Miss Daae's heart in his hands. Carlotta stood in the way of Christine's success for how many months? And while they have certainly felt your wrath, none of them has been openly threatened by death at your hands, nor have any of them been killed." I was almost to him.

"What is your point?"

"Simple. You have not killed any of these people, and I pose less of a threat than any of them. Why, then," I asked as I took my last step to be directly in front of him, "should I believe that you will kill me here, tonight?"

The Phantom looked at me and I had the sensation of being flung back in time, to the night of the Masquerade, standing on that precipice between war and peace. Enemies and friends. Life and death. I wondered, without Raoul here to interrupt it, how would it end?

Finally, Erik stepped back. "What would you have me do? Abandon everything I've worked for? Forget Christine? Perhaps you're going to tell me some other woman will fall in love with me!"

"No. No, I do not believe in giving someone false hope." The glimmer of superiority that sparkled in the Phantom's eye spurred me to continue. "So I will not give you false hope now. One thing the vicomte said tonight was true. How can Christine truly love you if you make her your prisoner? She will grow to resent you, eventually hate you and everything your world represents."

"No! I will give her everything! Everything the vicomte can and more!" Erik shouted, taking several more steps away from me.

"Are you quite sure of that?" I asked, raising my voice as well. When the echoes of our voices died down, I quietly asked, "What if she wanted to have a picnic in a field of flowers? Could you oblige her? What if she wanted a house in the city? Would you live so close to other people? What of her singing career? Yes, you are an expert teacher who has helped her voice tremendously, but should she succeed as a diva, she will be in the public eye. Could you bare that? What about dinner parties, cast parties, holiday affairs--"

"Enough!" Erik withdrew two sabres and their sheaths from underneath his cape. "If you will not come around to my way of thinking by persuasion, perhaps you will come by force!"

He tossed a sabre to me. I caught it, surprisingly dexterously, in my left hand. Even angered, the man was a fair sport, I had to admit. Now all I had to do was perform a reasonable facsimile of what I used to be able to do fencing-wise. A sabre was not a good choice to try this with, however. Duelling with a sabre meant fast and fluid footwork, something I did not possess, nor ever would again.

Erik immediately went on the offensive, jabbing and attacking with remarkable skill. Since I knew I had to rely so much on my cane, I merely blocked, trying to force him a few steps back. He was relentless, however, pushing me back towards the stairs.

"By force? Why can we not continue to talk? What truly comes of our duel?"

"A resolution. One of us will go ahead with their life, the other will be a defeated man. And I will not chance being the second, Detective!"

"Why do you say that so derisively? Would you like me to call you, merely, Musician?"

"A better question might be why you're not bothering to truly fight. The vicomte may have been a better opponent than you. I thought you had some mastery of the art when I challenged you."

Mentally, I was stumped. Had my expectations for myself lowered to the point that he would compare me to Raoul--with Raoul emerging more favourably? I chanced a glance at Watson and our eyes met. Something in his gaze reminded me of our conversation where he asked me why my physical shape seemed to enhance -- or hinder -- my mental state. Suddenly, I knew exactly what he meant and I knew he was right. I'd gone into this fight thinking that if I could not win with words, it would mean my death. Something that, before the accident, would have been a foreign and disturbing consideration for me. I'd gone in convinced that this cane was something I had to rely on, instead of my mastery of fencing and being able to compensate for my disability.

Perhaps I was at a disadvantage with the condition of my leg, but why should that hinder my true capabilities? I had studied swordplay for many years, I should know how to compensate and give Erik a true match. Perhaps the fast and fluid footwork could be used to my advantage. I would not have reason or chance to press more weight upon my right leg than it could hold.

That decision made, I blocked him and swung my sword out, removing the tip of his from its vantage point in such a way that forced him back several steps. With those precious seconds at my advantage, I stepped forward and, with my sword held straight out pointing at Erik, I lifted up my cane and threw it away. I heard it land somewhere in the orchestra pit and, putting most of my weight over my left leg, sent my own jab towards Erik.

He was surprised. "So you have decided to fight. I'm glad."

"I cannot just hand you a victory. If you are to win at all, you must work for it," I grunted as I dodged his blade. As long as I kept on my toes and was mindful that my right leg could not hold me for more than a second, I believed I would be sufficiently acceptable.

Thus it continued for several long minutes, one of us gaining the advantage and then losing it. Erik was an extraordinary fencer. I've never seen his equal. I was quite sure he could have bested me at any moment, so perhaps my initial impression that he would not hold back was erroneous. However, if that was indeed the case, I needed to end this soon; otherwise the Phantom might be tempted to fully loose his abilities. I was holding my own now, but I didn't know how I would fare if the Phantom's skill increased.

"Yes, we must work for all that is gotten in life," Erik commented, whether to continue our conversation, or just to remind himself of the fact, I'm not sure.

An opening. "Is that why you have this plan concerning *Don Juan Triumphant?*"

"And what do you know of my plans?"

"Simply that one exists," I fabricated. "I am rather curious about why, though. Why create the entire spectacle of a performance? If you want her, why have you not simply taken her?"

Erik laughed, even as he thwarted another of my attacks. "You actually have no ideas? Have you not noticed how closely everything within these magnificent prison walls correlates to me? It is a spit in my face! So I decided to have my own enjoyment with ironies. Have you actually read my opera? None of the singers will even realize what they're saying!"

I almost stopped moving. Erik was precisely correct. I had to wonder about his assumption that it was on purpose, but so many things within the opera house had to do with masks, hiding your true face, or some other similar theme. Why, a song I recalled hearing at the Masquerade had a line that said something about hiding your face so the world wouldn't find you.

"So you plan to trap her by having her sing an aria that she believes is nothing more than one character's sentiments toward another, when you're taking it to mean her feelings for you."

"When Christine reads them, she will know. Once she has spoken them, she cannot take them back. These are not just my words. They are the words I know we have longed to say to one another."

"Shouldn't Miss Daae have a say in that?"

Erik's eyes flashed dangerously and darkened in anger. I had to end this now. We were centre stage, near his chair, so I decided to use it against him. Lifting my left leg, I put my foot down on the seat and boosted myself up. With most of my weight still on my left leg, I brought my right foot up on the armrest and fought him over the back of the chair.

He quickly moved to the side so the back of the chair no longer separated us. His tactic somewhat surprised me. In a match like this, normally one would go to the opponent's back, attempting to gain the advantage. A somewhat underhanded manoeuvre, I admit, which is why the Phantom didn't take it, I suppose.

We continued to duel, swords clashing, the almost musical clang of metal on metal in our ears, when I slashed out in a thrust that Erik dodged. The blade whistled over his shoulder.

That was where my leg decided to give out on me. Or rather, I became too intensely involved in the fencing match and forgot that I had limitations unimaginable to me when I first learned the art. That thrust caused me to rest too much weight on my bad leg and it would not hold me. I crashed to the floor, hitting my right elbow hard enough to numb the appendage momentarily before a throbbing pain set in, and losing the sword in the process. Quickly, I turned over, my back against the chair's side, my left hand holding my right elbow, just as the Phantom stepped over and put his sword at my throat.

Fear coursed through me, but I remained vigilant in the face of such a being. Once again, the only weapons

I had were my words. I had to speak carefully, because even though I hoped he wouldn't, I knew the Phantom would kill me with no hesitation if he truly thought he needed to. I forced my face to reveal nothing and distantly hoped, once again, that the acting skills Watson spoke of me possessing were indeed as great as he always said. I could not afford to show fear now. Hoping that my next words would save my life, I opened my mouth. "My dear friend, you cannot best me. You may kill me, but my spirit will not be taken down by a mere mortal. And that is precisely what you are."

The Phantom's hand, which held the sword at my throat, wavered slightly. I watched the doubt enter his dark, melancholy eyes. My gaze remained unfaltering upon his masked face as finally, he looked away, took the sword from my neck, and tossed it. It clattered to the ground, skidded, and finally lay still at the edge of the stage.

As the echoes of its travel resounded, I took a deep breath, holding it when Erik turned back to look at me.

"Never," he rasped, "never has someone referred to me as merely a mortal. As far back as my memory can stretch, I have been a monster. A freak. A demon or devil."

Letting my breath out slowly, I carefully sat forward, taking my hand from my still throbbing elbow, and would have attempted standing, had my cane not been somewhere in the vast orchestra pit. "Erik," I said, "freaks or monsters, demons and devils, they are the products of imaginations. They are the projections people have placed on you. You needn't fall into that stereotype any longer."

"You know nothing of the stereotypes I've been plagued with!" the Phantom shouted. He grasped one of the many ropes that hung above both our heads and pulled. A trapdoor opened and he disappeared into its depths.

"Damn!" I cried, not daring to slide down into the passageway myself. "For lack of this chronic limp, I could follow him!"

After the Phantom disappeared, Watson found my cane and brought it to me.

"Thank you, Watson."

"Holmes, that was an incredible display. You were marvellous."

I gave him a sardonic grin. "You needn't flatter me, old boy." Getting to my feet, I looked at the still-open trap door and said, "Well, let's find out where this leads. Hopefully, it will be to his lair instead of to both our deaths. Unless, do you wish to stay here?"

"I would rather chance the Phantom's wrath to that of the policemen in this city."

"Agreed. Well, shall we make our descent?"

The only part of the lair I definitively remember from that period was the lake. It had several floating lanterns at strategic places across its vast surface. Watson and I used a small dinghy that must have been left for us by the Phantom to get across. I noted how many pillars, as well as lights, we passed on our twenty minute trip to the opposite shore.

We found the Phantom's lair open and carefully went inside. Erik must have heard our footsteps, because even before we saw him, we heard his voice.

"I've been waiting for you, Monsieur Holmes. I expected you to arrive sooner."

We approached him slowly, more because my leg was stiffening frightfully quickly than from any sense of caution.

Erik was sitting comfortably in an ornately

decorated silver and onyx chair, the wide brim of his hat shadowing most of his face and mask, the tips of his spindly fingers meeting in front of his deep eyes.

"I would like to have come sooner, but you see I'm somewhat impaired," I said, gesturing at my cane.

"There was no impairment to your skills during our fencing match."

"Touché. However, there was. I was compensating for my disability. You did have me at the end when I gave my leg more credit--and weight--than it could support."

"Even so, I have never met my equal in fencing. I'm sure I know why you've come, so shall we skip the needless formalities and go straight to our inevitable stalemate?"

"Then you know precisely what I come to request?"

"Indeed. A simple continuation of your plea that I sacrifice my plan during the performance of my opera."

I smiled, somewhat cruelly. "My dear Phantom, I do not plead with anyone. And, if my memory serves, I was not pleading for you to sacrifice anything. I was simply learning of your plan. Regardless, no. That is not why I come."

Those dark eyes widened in surprise and he sat back, putting his hands down. For once, he was thrown off-guard. "Then . . . Why?"

"I have done some thinking while Watson and I traversed your lake. I said above that Miss Daae should have a say in what you have planned for her. Yet I also acknowledge you have no way to accomplish that goal when she is on the surface, as it were. Go through with your plan. Bring her down here and present her with your choice. However, let me be present, as well, in your lair."

"You? Down here?" Erik lowered his hands and leaned forward. "An interesting concept. Why should I indulge you, though?"

"Nothing I can say will be any kind of threat to you. I ask that you indulge me out of friendship. Or, if you refuse to call me a friend, then out of mutual respect."

He sat back and nodded slowly. "You are no fool," he murmured, more thinking aloud than anything else. "No, I do not believe you're a threat to me. If that intent were present, you would have taken action by now to apprehend me. You surely would not have come alone and fenced with me, especially considering what you claim to be a disability. However," he looked at me, raising the volume of his voice, "when would you come down here?"

"The same time as you. Or slightly before." I smiled. "Erik, I'm genuinely curious about your opera. You would not ask me to come down here several hours before your abduction of Miss Daae and have me miss it, would you?"

"If I didn't know better, I'd say you sneaked down here and saw my plans. How is it that you have such a keen understanding of my mind?"

"Because as far as I can deduce, we are both geniuses forced to communicate with mediocre men on a daily basis. Now that I'm in the condition you see me, I can truthfully say we are both physically damaged for life. We both look more at the little details of situations to give us the bigger picture. And--" my voice broke. I swallowed deeply and continued. "We've both had such a profound love for a woman. A love that could mean our own destruction."

The Phantom stood and seemed to glide over to me. "Destruction? Is that where your drive comes from? Your analytical mind, your mental prowess, your resistance to mind games, it all stems from the total destruction of your own heart?"

I closed my eyes, her face swimming before my tightened eyelids for the first time in years. I whispered, "Yes."

"And you believe this same emotional devastation will befall me, should I take Christine?"

I met his eyes. "I believe it will befall you whether you take her or not. Erik, I will not deny she has feelings for you. I would be lying if I tried. I've seen with my own eyes that she cares for you, but I do believe it only extends as far as pity for your ruined face. She's intimidated by you. She claims you told her she can never be free. And the Masquerade . . . 'Your chains are still mine. You belong to me.'"

"She had no right engaging herself to that insolent fool. I disappeared for so long merely for the chance to complete my opera. And she acts as if I was dead!"

"Not dead. Simply one who released her." Then, it was as if a light turned on in my head. "The chandelier . . . I knew jealousy didn't make sense as the only reason to bring it down. You wouldn't destroy the opera house over so human and so illogical an emotion as that. It was never an accident. Nor a calculated decision fuelled by the anger you felt over what you heard on the rooftop. It was nothing more than a diversion!"

"Yes. It was only to be that, in the beginning. But after what I heard between Christine and that . . . *boy* . . . I decided to use it as a warning to her as well."

"Which she did not heed and that, in turn, spurred your actions at the Masquerade Ball." I put my hand to my forehead. "I have never met a foe with quite so layered an intellect."

"You are no slouch yourself. I doubt anyone else could have pieced together my plans and motives so well."

"I have you to confirm my thoughts," I countered.

"But the deduction was your own." He sighed, turning away from me, and walked over to a large, dark shape against the wall. Erik lit numerous candles in some of the most ornate candelabras I've ever seen. When he was done, I realized the hulking shape was an organ. He sat down and let his fingers drift over the keys. "You mentioned how masterfully I played the violin, Monsieur Holmes. Is my guess correct that you play as well?"

"I suppose, though I feel that after hearing you, I will be able to produce nothing but noise." I moved closer to the organ, until I was somewhere between it and the chair he'd been sitting in.

"Nonsense. How many Beethoven pieces are you familiar with?"

"Very few, which most find surprising. I'm more of a Bach-favouring man myself. His fugue in . . . blast, I can never recall if it's D or G minor is especially to my liking."

"Played on a pipe organ?" the Phantom inquired.

"Yes. For all my recollection of detail . . . Oh, well, it's a beautiful piece, the same melodies weaving in and out around each other. I've always had a fondness for it."

"As have I," Erik said, and began playing it. "Of course, I've also always loved the Moonlight Sonata."

"Ah, yes. One of the few Beethoven pieces I immensely enjoy."

"What about-t-t M-M-Mozart-t-t-t?" a voice behind and to my left stuttered.

I turned and saw Watson, looking nearly frozen, next to the chair the Phantom had initially been sitting in. "Watson! I'm so sorry, old boy, I'd completely forgotten you'd come."

The Phantom stood. "I'll get him some blankets from my private chamber."

I nodded my thanks and made my way over to Watson. "I'm sorry, you've been so quiet I scarcely remembered you were there. Why haven't you spoken up?"

"I suppose awe is as good an answer as any," he answered. "This p-place . . . When you talked of someone living down here, I . . . Well, I never d-d-dreamed it would look like this. B-b-be this b-big. Have separate rooms."

"The Phantom is a genius," I told him. "What more need be said?"

Watson nodded, though he still looked around in amazement. Erik soon came out with several blankets and instructed Watson to make himself comfortable. He tugged on an intricately braided rope that hung from the ceiling and a curtain was pulled back to reveal a bed with carvings of a swan in the headboard. "You may rest there if it's to your liking," Erik told Watson, who agreed and went over to stretch out on the cushion, covering himself in the blankets as he did.

"Thank you, Erik. I should have remembered,

Watson was stricken with a head cold the day after our arrival to Paris. Since his injury in Afghanistan, his ability to fully recover from things is nearly diminished."

"He undoubtedly remembers. If he knows a cold, airy space will affect him weeks after feeling unwell, why did he follow you?"

I smiled slightly. "He said he'd risk your presence than deal with the Parisian police. And to be fair, since we've never actually been in your dwelling, neither of us had any way to know it would be cold and airy."

Erik nodded. "I forget about the cold most times. There is a heating system I rewired for my lair, but more often than not, when I'm here, I'm composing. Those times, the candles and my own intensity are enough to keep me sufficiently warm."

"I've experienced that as well. Sometimes in the dead of winter, even after I would build a fire, I would barely be able to hold my violin, my fingers were so cold and cramped. But the more I played, the more vigorously my fingers extended until there were times I would extinguish the fire. It simply became too hot."

"Truly a fellow musician," he said appreciatively.

I took a few steps back toward his organ. "Might I

examine your dwelling, Erik?"

"That depends on what you hope to find," he answered.

"For once, nothing. I would just like the chance to explore the estate you've managed to build down here. For one thing, how many miles beneath the surface are we?"

"I believe the measurement came to four and a quarter. The lake was a huge help to me in that. Many people said Garnier was insane, wanting to dig so far down below the surface, let alone build so many caverns and such. No one would venture down that far, he was told. But then I gave him the reasoning that we'd have to dig this far for the lake to be drained, built around, and then replaced. If we tried to build right on top of it, eventually the foundation would sink. The opera house would not stand up to the test of time."

"It is a wonder," I said slowly, still trying to find the right words to express my thoughts, "that you are still able to put so much caring into a building, a piece of music, or a young girl. It is an absolute miracle that your life has not jaded you to the point of never having contact with human beings again."

"I have no explanations. Life for me has been one cruel twist of fate after another. It seems, though, when I'm on the brink of true madness, true despair, something comes along and pulls me back. Though never enough. Never enough."

"You expected Miss Daae to be your final salvation."

He looked at me. "Is it so wrong to want to be saved? That's why I appeared as her Angel of Music at first. I thought if I was nothing more than a storybook figure who came to her . . . But it wasn't enough. For either of us. And she begged to see me. I fled, thinking, knowing, she could never accept me. But she continued to plead with me, and I knew that wretched boy was waiting for her. She'd sung so beautifully, and I knew it was only to please me. So I brought her down here, singing to her even as I glided the boat over the waters. I told her of my love for her, told her how cruel the daylight world is, how I could take her places her dreams didn't dare take her.

"Exertion overcame her. She fainted in my arms. But I believed I'd gotten through to her. The next morning, though . . ."

The Phantom reached up and took off his mask. I

couldn't help it. I gasped at the skeleton-like visage before my eyes. Bile rose in my throat, but I choked it back, feeling its burn as it slid down my oesophagus.

His mask only covered the right side of his face, from forehead to chin, and his entire nose. The left side appeared almost ordinary, except for the skin looking abnormally pale, and blue veins prominently standing out near his temple. The right side, however . . .

His lip was a bulging mess, split and chapped on both upper and lower, some spots rippling upward to expose misshapen, crooked teeth. His lower lid seemed to have been melted like candle wax and oozed down his cheek, which was sunken and gaunt. Even his right ear, I now noticed, which was normally covered by his hair, was deformed. It folded in on itself and had the vague appearance of a small piece of cauliflower.

"She saw this when she came and took off my mask and I-- I flew into a rage. Perhaps, had I not done that-- But it's far too late now."

"Indeed," I replied when I felt I could competently speak. "Your face is . . ." I paused, not knowing what to say.

"A death's head. Skeleton face. Monster.

Demon. Devil. Or if you like the mundane, simply use 'ugly.'"

I closed my eyes, unable to hold back a slight laugh. Erik replaced his mask and gave me a sharp glare. "Why do you laugh?"

"I'm sorry. All the words you used to describe yourself and then, you're right, the rather mundane use of 'ugly.' I must admit, that word does not do you justice."

"Because my features are far beyond the mundane," Erik said.

I nodded, wondering if I'd offended him, but then I saw the slight upward curve of the left side of his lips. "It's interesting that you, someone so logical, so cold, would have a sense of humour."

"Perhaps a morbid one, but I do find ways to pull myself out of complete seriousness." I wandered closer to the organ and saw a small table behind it. On top, a figure of a monkey sat, dressed in Persian robes, holding a pair of cymbals. It was perched on a box covered in velvet. "This is exquisite," I commented.

The Phantom was behind me in a moment. "Ah, the music box. Yes, I created it during my stay in Persia. I was commissioned to build torture devices there and even my mind was taxed with ways to kill the ones deemed guilty. I had to find a way to counter the requests for torture chambers and this monkey came about as the answer." He picked it up and fiddled with something underneath. When he set it back down, the monkey stood up and banged its cymbals together in time to a tune.

"That music. I feel as though I've heard it before," I said softly.

"You have. It was the song I played in the cemetery."

"Yes, of course . . ." I began to hum along and then just as abruptly as it began, the monkey sat back down and movement and music ceased.

"Is it broken?" I asked.

"Broken?" Erik laughed. "Hardly. I've made this to last longer than a lifetime. Perhaps he does not like sharing the spotlight."

"Of course. I should have realized."

Erik and I met gazes. It seemed he realized he'd revealed more than he intended. We were at a mental stalemate. Since he'd told me more than I'd had any right to expect already, I decided to give him his desired space.

"I should get back to the hotel room. Watson

should be released from this damp atmosphere as well. As I mentioned, he caught a cold when we first came. I don't relish the thought of it coming back."

"Do you need assistance getting back?" Erik offered.

"Perhaps over the lake. After that, I believe I'm quite capable, thank you." My eyes fell on the monkey figurine again. "Erik, is there anything you wish me to do . . . up there? Can I assist you in any way, or shall I merely let them flounder in their own ignorance?"

"What would you do?" he asked.

"I'm not entirely sure. But it seems I could help you in some way."

"I don't think you can. However, I will help you. I assume you'll be in the audience for *Don Juan's* premiere?"

"Of course. As I said, I would not miss your opera."

"Do not attempt to get to the stage. I'll be using the same trapdoor I did tonight. There is another passageway, just outside Box three . . ." He proceeded to describe its location to me, as well as how the trigger mechanism worked. "I would lead you out using it, but you never know who's wandering around up there."

"Better we're led to the same entrance we used when coming in. If not for this cane, I'd be willing to chance it, but since I cannot walk silently . . ."

"Let us wake your friend, then."

Erik and I woke Watson and the three of us got into the boat. The Phantom led us out and Watson and I went back to our hotel room. It had been an exciting night and I'm certain that under normal circumstances, my leg hurting, or mind whirling would have kept me up for hours later. But mercifully, after I changed into a nightdress, tiredness overtook me and I fell into a deep sleep.

Don Juan Triumphant

Several weeks after Erik's and my swordfight and Watson's and my subsequent visit to his dwelling, *Don Juan Triumphant* was ready to be performed. When Watson went to speak with Andre and Firmin about our seating arrangement, I inspected the section of wall about ten feet away from Box Three. Much like the section of floor at the masquerade, there was only a thin line to indicate to the careful observer that there was anything there.

I tried the trigger mechanism some dozen times before it finally worked and I could see the path down to Erik's lair. Then, sneaking a furtive glance over each shoulder, I closed the passage and caned my way to the managers' office.

Watson was just leaving and I said to him, "You have assured our seating in Box Three?"

"Yes, though it was rather difficult. They insisted a guest near royalty status had already requested Box Three; however, I told them you wanted it because if the Phantom struck, it was the quickest route out of the opera and to the police."

"Brilliant, old chap!" I said. "And those buffoons who call themselves managers are gullible enough to fall for that ruse."

"Yes, I'm sure that ordinarily they would have been."

"Ordinarily? Why do you say 'ordinarily?'" I asked as we made our way outside into a cool Paris breeze.

"Well, they informed me that the police have been notified and the vicomte will be giving orders for Erik's capture that night."

"Damnation! That's right. The vicomte and his foolish notions of capturing our Ghost. How could it have slipped my mind?" I shook my head. "But you procured our seats?"

"Box Three, yes. It took a bit more doing, but they relented. Honestly, Holmes, why did you not just talk to them?"

"I needed them out of the way while I inspected Erik's passageway. He truly is ingenious. It's built directly into the wall. The trigger mechanism, I refer to. No one, not even I, would have recognized its existence had Erik not informed me."

Watson nodded, then looked back at the opera, such a grand building, housing an even grander man within its depths. ""Do you think he is quite safe?"

I smiled, somewhat vindictively. "Erik will not be caught, no matter how many score of policemen are pulled in. Their brute strength and guns are no match for his cunning and intelligence."

"I wasn't speaking of Erik, Holmes. I meant, will the vicomte come away from all this unharmed, either by the Phantom or by Christine?"

An interesting question. I found I had no answer.

"Monsieur Holmes! I'm so glad you could come!" Christine called to me when I exited Box Three.

After last minute touches were made on costumes, ankles were wrapped to prevent sprains, and throats were massaged or singers took to drinking their different secretive remedies, the opera was scheduled to be performed. The opening night was a Wednesday, and Watson and I made sure to come several hours before the performance began.

Once again, I had checked the passageway near

Box Three, but I dared not open it more than an inch, for fear someone would notice what I was doing. It's hard to be discreet with several score of stagehands, policemen, and actors around. Not to mention two pig-headed managers.

I had noticed, upon entering Box Three, that policemen were patrolling the perimeters, as well as the ends of the aisles closest to the stage. It amused me to see that they actually believed the vicomte's plan would work. Still smirking, I had turned away and left the Box, only to hear Miss Daae's voice to my left.

"Nothing could have kept me away," I answered. At the same time, I couldn't help thinking, *'And nothing will keep Erik away.'*

"Where will you be sitting? Close to the stage, I hope."

"Watson and I are seated here, in Box Three. I was checking to make sure it had adequate foot room. It's a precaution I must take now, I'm afraid. If I were to have to leave quickly, it would be rather impossible if I was sitting front row." Inwardly, I smiled. It seems this cane did have its uses.

"Yes, that's true. Well, I'm told the balconies give

a rather enjoyable view. All the same, I'm sure you will enjoy tonight."

"As am I," I agreed. "Tell me, my dear, are you completely comfortable with the lyrics in this opera?"

"Well, at first the range of the arias gave me difficulty. But after several rehearsals, I feel I've adequately mastered them."

Something in her tone told me she was purposely misunderstanding my question. But I decided to leave it be. Phantom or no, this was a big night for her, being the first time she was chosen for a lead role, instead of picked as a last minute replacement. I simply nodded and took her hands gingerly, saying, "Well, the best of luck to you tonight."

She curtsied and smiled, then turned to walk away. Watson found me still in front of Box Three and we went inside. Once seated, I leaned my cane against the wall and stretched out my leg. "You know, I'm sorry I never did one thing," I commented to Watson.

"And what's that, Holmes?"

"Procured some opera glasses. This is a very pleasant view, but a pair of those glasses would help immensely."

"Would you like to use mine?" he asked, pulling a pair out of the inner breast pocket of his jacket.

"Thank you." I had an ulterior motive for the glasses. Erik as good as told me that he would take part onstage in his opera. I wanted to know who he would replace and when he would appear.

Not ten minutes after we sat down, the orchestra began tuning up and several harsh notes blared forth. I took out my pocket watch and saw it was still over an hour till the curtain was to rise. As I replaced the watch, I noticed Raoul talking to several of the policemen, one of whom was undoubtedly the chief. I watched them with interest. The vicomte pointed at the stage and then at the man's gun. He was about to make some other gesture when a voice shouted, "Secure!"

Raoul looked in the direction of the call and nodded determinedly. They must have been preparing for the lockdown within the opera after the guests arrived, assuming that Erik would try to take Christine out to the streets. Fools. Complete and utter fools. I shook my head in disappointment. Watson eyed me strangely and I pointed out the scene unfolding below. Andre and Firmin had joined the group and I was able to catch some of what they were saying to the police chief.

"They have their instructions, sirs, don't worry. My men are the best this city has ever had."

"Firmin, are you sure this will work?"

"Do you have another plan?"

"These doors are secure, sir!" someone else called from backstage.

"He won't get out, sirs. After the audience is in, we'll make sure no one can escape."

Raoul nodded and looked at someone in the orchestra pit. I leaned forward as far as I dared to hear what he would say. Unfortunately, their voices didn't carry up to my ears.

But not ten seconds later, a voice came from somewhere below and to the right of my balcony.

"I'm here . . . The Phantom of the Opera . . ."

All of the policemen turned around, pointing their guns toward the voice in a panic. Raoul shouted something and gestured violently for them to maintain their positions. The police chief agreed, yelling at them to act like professionals and quickly get into position. Several more times, the Phantom's disembodied voice came from different areas of the giant room. It rattled them, but surprisingly, none of the guns went off. Perhaps they were better trained than I'd given them credit for.

When all was silent for a few minutes, the orchestra went back to tuning and the announcement was made that the audience would be let in, which leads me to believe I'm the only one who heard the soft laughter coming from what seemed to be right over my shoulder, and the cold voice say, *"Yes, let the audience in and let my opera begin!"*

I listened to the first act, though I had a difficult time following. Blast Erik, even before I confirmed as much in his lair, he must have known I would decipher his lyrics for hidden meanings. The lyrics were sung in Italian, a language I only minimally follow.

Twenty minutes in, I despaired understanding the singers and instead chose to focus on who was onstage.

Piangi's and Carlotta's characters were warbling to one another when I spotted someone behind a piece of scenery. I grabbed the opera glasses in order to get a better look, but when I had them to my eyes, he was already gone.

"The Phantom," I chanced to breathe.

Watson heard me and leaned over. "Holmes, are you sure?"

"Indeed. He will show himself again," I answered grimly.

During the intermission between acts, I felt the need to stretch my legs. I excused myself and left Box three to walk briefly up and down the corridor. It was on this small excursion that I saw Andre and Firmin leaving the washroom.

"Well, gentlemen," I said as I approached them, "It seems the police force you've set up has sufficiently intimidated the Phantom."

There was a pause, where I'm sure both men were ascertaining whether or not sarcasm was in my tone.

"Indeed," Andre replied cautiously. "There have been no mishaps and we're almost ready for the second act. The 'Phantom' would be foolish to act now."

I nodded, but as I turned away, I murmured under my breath, "Would he?"

When I was back in my seat, Watson turned to me questioningly.

"Andre and Firmin think the Phantom will not strike."

"I take it you corrected them of their erroneous hope?"

"No. Let them flounder. They have put their faith in the vicomte. I've placed mine in Erik. We shall see whose was the wiser choice."

Watson nodded and we both turned to look at the stage as the lights dimmed and the orchestra began playing. As the opera came to its climax, I was surprised to hear English lyrics from the character onstage.

Do you know whose arms you dwell in tonight,
you fair, fair, mistress of the morn?
Tis I, you wench! One who's suffered
since the day he was born!

I barely dared to breathe. I motioned to Watson to look at that figure, swathed in black robes. We could tell nothing of his physique, but of course, that was the plan. The voice, however, was unmistakable. The Phantom had taken centre stage.

Unfortunately, I missed several lines of his aria

while my attention wandered to a few stray facts and questions. First and foremost on my worried mind was the location of Piangi -- the man who should have been in those robes. Second was what would happen if any of those fools below realized something was amiss. If a policeman should shoot at someone onstage, they could miss and hit a stagehand, or another singer. Third, I noted this when I gave a quick sweep of the theatre, *no one else realized what I knew!*

As his aria came to a close, Christine and the Phantom twirled around the stage in their macabre and provocative dance -- appropriately titled 'Dance of Death' in the performance program. Two thoughts struck me simultaneously as I watched. First, how awkward the dance must have been for Piangi, considering his girth, and second, Christine would soon know she was not dancing with him.

That realization was instantaneous. One second, Christine was wholly immersed in her character, a beautiful and seductive smile playing across her face; the next, Erik's cowl must have shifted, because her expression filled with horror and fear.

She stopped dancing, but was unable to back more

than an arm's length away. The Phantom still held her wrist. I leaned forward as the music stopped and a confused hush came over the crowd.

"Christine . . ."

Her gaze was one of a woman who could not tear her eyes away even if every fibber of her being was crying for her to do so. She glanced down at her wrist, the one Erik still held. When he made no move to release her, she stepped closer to him, resting her hand on the side of the cowl over his face. In one fluid movement, he was exposed.

The audience below seemed to gasp in unison, and several people cried out, "The Phantom!"

I chanced a look at Andre and Firmin. Both were standing at attention, hands ready to signal the police, eyes on the stage. The vicomte was behind them, a stricken expression playing on his features. I could imagine his thoughts. All of his careful planning, all his precautions, all his hopes to outwit the Phantom, completely for naught. Once again, Erik showed cunning far beyond what his adversaries expected of him.

"Say you love me, Christine.

I can give you everything.

Just give me the chance,

Let our love dance,

Let me be beside you as you roam.

Christine, let me give you a place to call--"

Christine had begun to caress his face as he sang, but just before he reached the last word, she tore the mask off his face, exposed his horrid visage to the world. Erik let out a scream that drowned out everyone else's and swirled his cape around Christine. Before anyone could react, they dropped through the trapdoor on the stage.

"That clever devil!" I shouted, standing and grasping the rail. "Watson, come. We must catch up with him."

We quickly made our way into the corridor and I opened the passageway. Luckily, in their panic, everyone was headed downstairs to the exits. Almost no one was in the hallway with Watson and myself. Which is undoubtedly how I heard Madame Giry so clearly as we stepped into the passageway.

"Monsieur La Vicomte, follow me!"

I quickly closed the door behind us and breathed a small sigh of relief that we weren't seen. However, I now knew we had another problem.

"I should have foreseen it, Watson, but soon there will be another 'guest' in the Phantom's lair."

We trod forward carefully over the uneven ground of the passageway, until our efforts brought us to a pit.

"I should have known he wouldn't make things easy. Watson, you have your bag with you?"

"Yes," Watson replied, holding it out. I took it, opened it, and began rummaging through the supplies I'd put in that morning.

"Holmes, what--?" Watson said incredulously as I lit us a torch.

""I knew we would need supplies, but it was imperative to remain discreet."

Slowly I swept the torch from one wall to the other. Along the left side of the pit was a ledge, about a foot's width wide, leading to the other side.

"Watson, if you can tiptoe across, I know how we can proceed." I pointed out the ledge to him.

His eyes widened and his skin paled, but he nodded resolutely. "But Holmes, how will you--?"

"Make sure your attempt brings you safely across, my friend. Then I shall explain my method."

When Watson had safely crossed, I threw his bag over to him and instructed he take out the length of rope inside.

"Tie one end around your waist, or perhaps one of the bigger boulders behind you. Then, toss me the other end."

"Holmes, you can't mean to tell me you intend to jump across!"

"Indeed, I intend to do just that. I won't make it, which is why I'll have the rope tied around me. I hope to make enough of a leap that I will be able to grasp the opposite edge. Then, you pull me the rest of the way up."

Watson sighed, but nodded. "Understood. Be careful, Holmes."

"Always. Now, throw me the rope."

After things were properly set up, Watson held the rope with very little slack and I tossed him my cane and limped up to the edge. Using my left leg, I sprung myself out over the abyss. The airborne feeling I had in those few seconds lasted a lifetime, and I found myself feeling freer than I had in a very long time. But it ended far too soon, and my arms and chest collided with the opposite edge. All the air exploded from my lungs in the form of a single, large gasp and for a moment I could neither inhale nor feel my arms. I have no doubt I would have fallen to my death had Watson not been there to grab my shoulders and pull me to safety.

Once we were both on solid ground and I could breathe again, he handed me my cane and helped me to my feet.

"Holmes, you're as daring as ever," was all he said as we proceeded down the corridor.

I smiled to myself.

Erik's path led us to somewhere behind his lair. I figured out the way in, but wanted to approach him from the front. So Watson and I subjected ourselves to lake water as we made our way to a thick wooden gate with a boat just outside it.

"Watson, you stay here. Be ready in the boat in case a quick escape is needed. I will proceed on foot and try to keep some sanity to the outcome."

Watson nodded and grasped my shoulder briefly. "Be careful, Holmes."

"Of course."

As I slowly sloshed up to the gate through calf-high water, I heard voices within. I raised the gate just enough to slip under comfortably and lowered it quietly. When I gazed toward the organ with the multitude of lit candelabras, I saw Christine and Erik arguing.

"Have you had your fill of men's blood? Do you now wish to take me, have your fill of the joys of my flesh?"

"Fate has condemned me and denied me the joys of a woman's body. However, I told you that you belong to me. Down here, you have no choice! No one will save you!"

"I wouldn't be too sure of that," I commented lightly as I splashed closer to them.

"Ah, but Monsieur Holmes, you said you wanted to be present, not join in the festivities."

"Perhaps, but you speak only of her belonging to you," I said, deciding my best course of action was to place myself in the thick of things. "What of your previous declarations of love?"

"Indeed, what of those?" Christine added. "You would not have me be your wife, you would have me be your prisoner!"

"If you truly love her, what stands between you?" I asked, wishing Miss Daae had remained silent.

"This face!" Erik yelled, his answer reverberating through walls and eardrums alike. "My face! It earned my mother's hatred. Did you know my first pitiful scrap of clothing was a mask?" Erik's eyes had been switching between myself and Christine. When he saw her sad, sympathetic expression, he whirled on her, his cloak forming a wide arc around him. "Your pity comes far too late, my dear. The price of your treachery is an eternity of *this* before your eyes."

Christine's eyes flickered away, but then met Erik's resolutely. "Your ruined face is no sight of horror for me now. The true distortion lies within your soul."

The two looked at one another for what seemed like an eternity. Once again, I wonder what could have been altered in the coming events if it weren't for the absolutely dreadful timing of the vicomte.

I believe Erik and I heard the splashes and gurgling at the same time because something broke in his hopeful gaze at Christine. His eyes narrowed and he glanced at the wooden gate, Raoul's only chance at entry from the underground lake. I was happy to see Watson was out of sight.

"Wait, my dear," he snarled. "I think we have a guest."

Soundlessly, an impressive feat since he had to walk through water, he approached the gate. When Raoul, so fixated on Christine, reached through the bars to try and find a lever to raise the gate, the Phantom grabbed his arm. Raoul screamed and stared, wide-eyed, into the Phantom's fully exposed face.

"Sir," Erik began, a mockery of the polite society which was the vicomte's world, "this is indeed a most pleasurable delight. I'd hoped you could join us. Since you have most adequately obliged, it has truly made my night!"

The vicomte's expression turned to terror, yet he held his ground. Determination entered his eyes as he implored Erik.

"Free her! Do whatever else you want, but please, free her! Monsieur, have you truly no pity?"

Erik let go of Raoul's wrist and whirled around to face Christine, who had cowered behind me. "Your lover's plea is almost sincerely passionate."

Christine called to Raoul that his words were useless.

Addressing first Christine, then Erik, Raoul answered, "I love you! Does that mean nothing? I love her, please, there must be some mercy in you. Show us some compassion."

Had the Phantom's response not been so full of pain or said so bitterly, I could have laughed at the idea of Raoul begging for compassion from the man he'd previously wanted dead.

"This earth holds no compassion for me."

As his last word echoed throughout the chamber, a horrified expression settled over the visage of the vicomte. For once, not horror by Erik's deformity; instead, horror at the idea of what he must have gone through because of such a face.

I barely dared to breathe, I didn't dare move. Raoul's mouth opened and I found myself hoping, for a brief instant, that rationale would take over and he would stop blubbering and retreat from the gate.

But Christine moved, rippling the water at her ankles, and Raoul's attention shot to her, his eyes once again holding only disdain for the Phantom.

"Let me see her," Raoul growled, once again returning to the attitude of pure royalty, someone who expected to be obeyed without question. "Let me hold her. Let me know that you have done her no harm."

I anticipated that the Phantom would laugh in his face. Instead, Erik raised the gate and let Raoul enter. As the vicomte ran to Christine, I saw my chance to intercept.

"Miss Daae, on more than one occasion, you've heard the vicomte's declarations of love and devotion. Be fair to both men and listen to Erik's."

Both Christine and Erik looked at me with something akin to, simultaneously, fascination and fear. But the vicomte only scoffed.

"This is absurd!" he cried. "What ever can someone like *that--?!*"

"Vicomte!" I yelled, holding my cane out at him threateningly. "I will thank you to kindly keep your mouth shut. This is Erik's time to speak and since we are in his dwelling, I suggest you act in a courteous manner. Unless you prefer being tied up."

Raoul looked as though he was going to protest, but one glance at the Phantom, who had produced a rope seemingly out of thin air and was holding it taut between his hands, kept him silent. Meekly, the vicomte nodded and stepped back from Christine, once again into knee-deep water.

"Very good. Now, Erik, you have exposed your heart thus far with your actions. Please let Christine be privy to the rest of it. Speak what is in your heart. Because I'm sure that declarations of love hold more sway than the threat of capture and imprisonment."

Erik opened his mouth in an attempt to speak, but for all his eloquence in music, he could not seem to find the words now.

We stood in silence as Erik struggled. I hoped he could find the words soon, because the vicomte looked much like a volcano ready to erupt. Finally, when I doubt his face could have turned any redder, Raoul grasped Christine's shoulders and said, "That's it. I'm taking her away from this place! You have tortured her long enough, you'll do it no longer! You're a monster and nothing more!"

The Phantom's eyes flashed and I knew, one way or another, Raoul was doomed. Anger, Erik knew how to express with no hesitation. And he did so. Almost before Raoul could make a sound, his hands were tied behind his back and a lasso was around his neck. The Phantom dragged him backwards and slung the rope over one of the higher horizontal beams of the gate, tying it in such a way that forced Raoul onto his toes.

"Stop!" Christine cried, falling to her knees. "Erik, please . . . Please, stop. This isn't right. Raoul has done nothing to you, he's just in love with me. He cannot help wanting me for himself, just as I cannot help having no desire to choose between two men who are proclaiming their love for me."

"No desire to choose?" Erik mimicked. "I think you have a very strong desire to choose. As a matter of fact, I believe you already made your choice, my dear. But as I told you earlier, down here, it is only my choice that matters. And my choice remains that you belong to me!"

"Erik . . ."

"You betrayed me!" the Phantom yelled, pulling on Raoul's rope slightly, so that he choked a bit more. "You gave your love to the vicomte, to this fool, *and you were going to leave me!* It was only the chandelier's destruction that held you to the opera house. You knew if you ran I would find you."

Erik turned to Raoul. "Order your fine horses now, monsieur. You should have kept your hand at the level of your eyes. After all, you saw what happened to Joseph Buquet. This was exactly how he died, though his death was much quicker and less painful than I will make yours."

"Erik," I began calmly, "is this truly the way to win her love?"

"Love," he spat. "What does love matter anymore? You were right, Detective. The complete annihilation of my own heart. I should have listened to you." He turned away from me, but not before I saw tears glistening in his eyes. "I should have . . . I should . . . have listened . . ."

"Erik . . ." I approached him, not even sure what I intended to do. When we were face to face, I put my hand on his shoulder so our conversation would be unheard, and implored him. "Let Raoul go. He is beneath you. He is not worth you losing such a fine mind. Your life is worth living, Erik, I--"

Erik shrugged roughly out of my grasp and snarled. "This is no life that I have. And it isn't worth continuing, should I lose Christine." He turned to her.

"Christine . . ."

But for once, Christine's face had a hard, cold expression. "When I first saw your face, I cried. I wept that you should have the voice of an angel, yet suffer such a horrible fate. But now, any tears I would cry are tears of *hate!*"

Silence descended over the lair. The Phantom, Raoul, and I looked at her in shock. "Christine--" Raoul began.

"No, Raoul. Say nothing. You shouldn't have come here. I shouldn't be here. But you insisted I sing in his opera. You even threatened to leave me, should I listen to my own mind and not perform! I should have let you leave, because you were wrong! I was not safe. And now, we're down here, where we must play by *his* rules." She gestured roughly at Erik.

"Christine . . ." Erik began softly. "I simply wanted to be saved. To be loved. I-- I only ever wanted . . ." his voice trailed off as he tried unsuccessfully to hold back sobs.

I went to move closer to him, but something came over Christine's face then, and she stepped closer to Erik.

"Monsieur Holmes, please," Christine said, gently

touching my shoulder. I glanced at her and, seeing the resolution in her eyes, backed away.

"Inside, you're such a beautiful creature, despite being plagued by darkness. What kind of lonesome life have you known?" Christine sighed, a tear rushing down her jaw line and rested on her chin for a moment, before falling onto her heaving breast. "I now have the courage to show you you're not alone."

Christine inched closer to the Phantom even as he slowly backed away, and it seemed as if everyone in the room held their breath for that tense moment when the two stood face-to-face. Chorus girl turned diva and Opera ghost turned fearful child. Slowly, ever so slowly, Christine's arm came up and her hand grasped the back of the Phantom's neck. Carefully, gently, she guided his face down to hers and then wrapped her other arm around him and kissed his misshapen mouth.

Erik's fingers gnarled into something akin to claws, as if he wasn't sure whether to push her away or draw her closer. His indecision didn't last long; their lips still together, he lifted her up effortlessly, cradling her against his chest. My eyes strayed as I heard a choked sound of disgust. I glared at the vicomte, hoping that I was properly conveying the message that if he did anything to interrupt this union, no matter how grotesque he may find it, that he and Christine would undoubtedly never leave here together or alive. I assume he deciphered the gist of my meaning, because he swallowed thickly and turned his face away.

When the kiss ended, the Phantom stared at Christine with such love and devotion that *I* almost gagged. It still amazed me that such talented men, such shining geniuses of the mind could be brought to the level of snivelling children by the wiles or ways of a woman. Betrayed by their own hearts, which marched to completely different drumbeats than that of their minds, they strove to be something worthy of that woman.

Though a question nagged at the recesses of my consciousness. Was this a ploy of Christine's, in order that she and her precious vicomte might escape? Or had she finally seen how much Erik suffered and for once felt actual love for him instead of pity? Or was it pity and sympathy that guided her actions now? I felt I could have discerned something from her face, had I been able to see her expression, but her back was to me. I sighed soundlessly, hoping that whatever her reasons for the kiss, the end result would be our freedom.

"Christine," the Phantom murmured, bringing his skeletal hand up and caressing the side of her face. "Do you truly love me?"

"I love . . ." she began, but her voice faded away. "I loved you as my Angel. My guardian. The one who taught me to sing and gave me the confidence to use my talents in front of an audience. I even found I loved you as the mysterious Opera Ghost who soundlessly travelled the theatre, sometimes leaving destruction in your wake, because I knew those 'accidents' had a purpose. A purpose meant for me, that you would see your dream and mine come true, and that I would be a diva.

"But Erik, you set up such an ethereal connection between us. You were a spirit. A disembodied voice in my dressing room mirror. A messenger from Heaven, sent by my father. Or so I believed. But you were so much more and, at the same time, so much less, than just a man.

"I beg you to understand, Erik. You're my Phantom, my Guardian Angel, and in some ways, my God. You were meant to watch over me, protect me, and you have done this. But we were never meant to be. I'm meant to be with Raoul, for even though he is a petulant child compared to you, I see him as a man."

"But do you love me?" Erik persisted. I knew what he hoped to hear, yet at the same time, I couldn't help wondering why he chose to torture himself this way.

Christine looked away and closed her eyes, taking a deep breath. It was obvious she wanted to know the truth of her words before responding. When she opened her eyes, the expression they revealed told me she'd found her answer. She met Erik's eyes and said, "I will never love anyone the way I loved, and love, you."

Erik's lids fell shut and I saw the faint glimmer of a tear on his misshapen cheek. "Take her," he said, barely above a hoarse whisper. "Go. Now. I've gone too far with my stunts and traps. They will hunt me. Take her and go, forget about me and what you've seen here tonight."

Raoul didn't need to be told twice. He struggled against the ropes that bound him until Erik reached forward and cut one, releasing him from the other coils. Then Raoul lunged forward and grabbed Christine's hand, pulling her away from Erik. Though she went willingly, her eyes never left the Phantom. Raoul practically picked her up and placed her in the boat they would use to get across the lake, and I saw no need to tell them about the passageway Watson and I had used.

I watched Erik limp over to the chair and collapse on its seat. "Erik, I--"

"Holmes," he said, using my name for the first time, to my recollection, "leave me. Destruction of my heart, indeed. That woman--"

"Erik." This was becoming a contest of who would interrupt faster. "That 'woman' is an innocent girl who could not fathom the implications of being with someone of your intellect."

He gave something of a snort. "Intellect? You want me to believe she left, left with that wretched boy, because my *intellect* was intimidating her?"

I sighed, approaching him slowly. "No, I suppose I can't expect you to believe something so clearly make believe. I apologize for attempting to hide the more obvious reasons. However, I do hold to the idea that her mind was no match for yours. Undoubtedly you would have grown bored and restless with no one to contend with on an intellectual basis."

Erik glanced at me sharply. "What are you proposing, Detective?"

"I have never met your equal in brains or cunning. And the idea of having someone like you to help me is an enthralling concept. Erik, please, become my partner."

He looked up at me, an unreadable expression in his eyes. "You would ask me this? Ask me to join you in London society?"

"I would ask you to join me in my cases. I know now after this entire affair that the one with the vastly growing reputation of 'England's greatest detective' cannot lightly say he will retire. Yet I do not deny that I will need help if I am truly to solve more cases. More help than even Watson can give me, because while he is an intelligent man, he does not have our aptitude for sniffing out clues."

Once again, Erik closed his eyes. He rested his forehead on his waiting palm. "I can't. I'm sorry, Holmes, but I won't grant you this. The opera house is my home, my sanctuary, and my prison. I'm not leaving it."

"Erik, I--"

He stood up and grabbed my shoulders, practically throwing me towards the lake and the still open gate. I landed unceremoniously in water deep enough to cushion my fall. The Phantom strode up and pushed me again, so that he could close the gate between us.

Using the gate to assist me, I stood and faced him. "Erik, don't be so rash! I can protect you. They won't harm you, they'll--"

But then I heard it. Closer now, the march of angry people, yelling, demanding to find the Phantom's lair and put an end to his miserable existence once and for all. Yelling for revenge for Buquet and Piangi, and vowing that they refused to be victims anymore. The Phantom had to be run out.

"Go. Take the left passage once you're on the lake. You'll avoid the mob. You needn't be involved in what they wish to do."

"Erik . . ." For all my wit, for all my cunning, for all my blasted intelligence, why could I not think of anything meaningful to say? In desperation, I said, "Erik, your life is worth living. Please, don't throw it away. Not only have I considered you a worthy adversary and a man deserving of respect for his remarkable mind and musical ability, but . . . I consider you a cherished friend."

Erik didn't respond; he merely stared at me one last time as he went back to sit in his seat, swirling his cloak around him as he did until I no longer saw even the top of his misshapen head. There was nothing more I could say. Nothing more I could do. Sighing heavily, feeling like an absolute failure, I turned my back on the gate and climbed into the boat with Watson. We took Erik's advice and went down the left passageway, just in time to avoid the mob coming from the right. Echoes of yells and splintering wood haunted me as we made our way back to the surface.

From the Journal of John H. Watson, M.D.

It was an interesting journey, from London to Paris, from above the stage to miles below it in the depths of the city. A grand adventure to all but those who lived it.

As I thought back on our time in and under the Opera Populaire, Holmes drew his bow over the strings in a long, drawn-out note. My hands came together, clapping, before I realized it, and Holmes opened his eyes in surprise.

"Watson!" he exclaimed, holding his bow and violin in one hand while taking his cane with the other. "What a pleasure. Mrs. Hudson told me this morning you've been visiting every day."

"Since our return from Paris," I confirmed.

"Tell me, how long has that been?" he asked as he took a seat.

"Some months, I'm afraid. We've been very worried about you."

He gave me a rueful smile. "I'm sure taking time out of your day to see me did not please your wife."

"Neither pleased nor displeased. She's very understanding and realizes your welfare means a great deal to me."

"Thank you. And please make mention to her that I'm grateful for her understanding."

I nodded my agreement. "Have you made peace with the events in Paris?"

"Better than peace, my good man! Earlier today, Mrs. Hudson came in with a letter that immensely raised my spirits." He stood and caned his way over to an end table next to the couch. He picked up a piece of paper, folded in thirds, and handed it to me. "Here. Please, read this. Enormously good news, don't you think?"

I glanced down and saw faintly familiar writing scrawled across the page:

Sherlock Holmes,

I protected myself from the mob, hiding in another cellar behind the opera house. After they left, I attempted to stay in Paris, under the Opera Populaire, but I find I cannot. It holds far too many memories. With only the recollections of Christine left to me, I previously would have just let myself die. You have banged that, sir. So I come to you. It should be the 21ˢ when you receive this letter. I shall arrive the following day.

You told me my life was worth living. You called me a friend. I hold you to that claim now. My life is yours. Make it worth my living it.

Erik

P.S. You are also a cherished friend.

"Why, Holmes, is this genuine? What on earth does he mean?"

""It means that we shall have a familiar houseguest very soon."

"Do you mean to tell me Erik is alive?"

"Indeed. I was afraid I'd failed, that he wouldn't take my words to heart. But it seems he has. Erik is alive. And he's coming to London."

I admit, I was very shocked by Holmes's revelation concerning Erik. I knew nothing of their conversation in the lair, but was immensely glad to hear that Erik wouldn't throw his life away and that Holmes's words had a good deal to do with it.

Throughout the course of the rest of that day, in preparation for Erik's arrival, Holmes told me of the events that happened while I waited in the boat. I found, even as I was hearing them, that questions kept cropping up in my mind. Such as, if Erik truly desired Christine, why didn't he simply kill Raoul? He was definitely intelligent enough to make it look like an accident that had happened by chance. What would have changed if he had? Why did Christine kiss him and why would that change Erik's mind? Was the kiss a ploy on Christine's part? A last, desperate attempt for her and her lover to go free? Did she tell Erik the truth? Did she truly love both men, just in profoundly different ways?

The only thing I knew for sure was that Holmes and Erik understood one another. I used to question that as well. But that query, I once voiced to Holmes. He explained to me the same conclusion I'd come to around the time of their swordfight. They were both remarkably similar men, outcasts of, yet so well-known within, their worlds. Then he said to me, "Perhaps I don't have quite the physical deformity he does," and at that point, he looked down at his right leg and his hand gripping the cane. Then he continued, "but then, even as I say that, I wonder . . . aren't we all maimed?"

Coming Soon

This is the first in a series of Sherlock Holmes novels from Kate Workman. To keep updated on the news on Kate's books visit www.mxpublishing.com and subscribe to our newsletter which features the latest information and offers from our Holmes writers around the world.

Also from MX Publishing

Close To Holmes

A Look at the Connections Between Historical London, Sherlock Holmes and Sir Arthur Conan Doyle.

Eliminate The Impossible

An Examination of the World of Sherlock Holmes on Page and Screen.

The Norwood Author

Arthur Conan Doyle and the Norwood Years (1891 - 1894)

www.mxpublishing.com

Also From MX Publishing

In Search of Dr Watson

Wonderful biography of
Dr. Watson from expert Molly Carr.

Arthur Conan Doyle, Sherlock Holmes
and Devon

A Complete Tour Guide and
Companion.

The Lost Stories of Sherlock Holmes

Eight more stories from the pen of John H
Watson – compiled by Tony Reynolds.

www.mxpublishing.com

Also From MX Publishing

Watsons Afghan Adventure

Fascinating biography of Watson's time in Afghanistan from US Army veteran Kieran McMullen.

Shadowfall

Sherlock Holmes, ancient relics and demons and mystic characters. A supernatural Holmes pastiche.

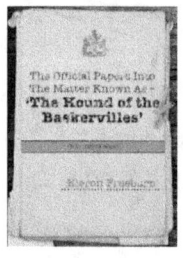

Official Papers of The Hound of The Baskervilles

Very unusual collection of the original police papers from The Hound case.

www.mxpublishing.com

Also From MX Publishing

The Sign of Fear

The first adventure of the 'female Sherlock Holmes'. A delightful fun adventure with your favourite supporting Holmes characters.

A Study in Crimson

The second adventure of the 'female Sherlock Holmes' with a host of sub-plots and new characters joining Watson and Fanshaw

The Chronology of Arthur Conan Doyle

The definitive chronology used by historians and libraries worldwide.

www.mxpublishing.com

Also From MX Publishing

Aside Arthur Conan Doyle

A collection of twenty stories from ACD's close friend Bertram Fletcher Robinson.

Bertram Fletcher Robinson

The comprehensive biography of the assistant plot producer of The Hound of The Baskervilles

Wheels of Anarchy

Reprint and introduction to Max Pemberton's thriller from 100 years ago. One of the first spy thrillers of its kind.

www.mxpublishing.com

Also From MX Publishing

Bobbles and Plum

Four playlets from PG Wodehouse 'lost' for over 100 years – found and reprinted with an excellent commentary

The World of Vanity Fair

A specialist full-colour reproduction of key articles from Bertram Fletcher Robinson containing of colour caricatures from the early 1900s.

Tras Las He huellas de Arthur Conan Doyle (in Spanish)

Un viaje ilustrado por Devon.

www.mxpublishing.com